WHEN GOD WENT TO HELL

WHEN GOD WENT TO HELL

Ravi Gupta

olive turtle

NIYOGI BOOKS

Published by

NIYOGI BOOKS

Block D, Building No. 77,
Okhla Industrial Area, Phase-I,
New Delhi-110 020, INDIA
Tel: 91-11-26816301
Email: niyogibooks@gmail.com
Website: www.niyogibooksindia.com

Editor: Sucharita Ghosh
Design: Shraboni Roy

ISBN: 978-93-85285-76-9
Publication: 2017

Printed at: Niyogi Offset Pvt. Ltd., New Delhi, India

To my friend, companion and wife...
Zarin

Contents

Foreword...9

Prologue...13

St Peter's Presentation...17

The Appointment of Consultants...38

The Functioning of Heaven...70

R&D's Report...87

Discussions on the Report...99

The Appointment of a CEO...105

God's Visit to Hell...123

Back in Heaven...149

Glossary...167

Acknowledgements...168

Foreword

I have always enjoyed new perspectives to existing beliefs and points of views. It is refreshing when existing perceptions are questioned and even challenged. It is this that I found so very interesting about Osho and I did end up spending some time at the Ashram to understand the man and his philosophy. But Osho himself believed that 'Philosophy, the very word means love for wisdom, and it has nothing to do with wisdom at all. Wisdom happens only through meditation; it never happens by collecting information.' Osho further adds, 'The moment you start thinking you follow the path of logic.' The pragmatic and practical approach to issues of life and his responses on how we should deal with them in our day-to-day life is what was most impressive about him.

As an educationist myself it has always been my endeavour to get students not just to accumulate information and knowledge, but to question, think and analyse. To this purpose I have also introduced 5th Veda at Whistling Woods International as a concept of learning through questioning, interacting, analysing with masters of the industry while at the same time meditating which helps in crystallising the thought process and bringing about internal peace that is so needed to gain wisdom. Challenging existing established notions and belief systems has helped evolve the human mind and always brought about changes in the society whether culturally, economically or socially. Any society that is not open to change or not willing to experiment can never hope to progress. Discussion, debate and disputes are central to emergence of new thoughts. It is not essential that there needs to be agreement.

I was therefore pleasantly happy to come across a book that was willing to look at afterlife in a totally new perspective and in the process challenge many well-grounded beliefs. Interestingly it is the Characters themselves who question the narrative of the writer, including their very existence, that makes us think. Heaven and Hell are well-grounded concepts with little known of either of them beyond macro level perceptions. The concept of Heaven and Hell are both pragmatic and meaningful creations whether they actually exist or are only a creation of the human mind. If they do indeed exist how exactly would they function? Could Heaven be a Company servicing its clients? Or a Trust serving the deserving? Or as generally perceived, a paradise rewarding souls who have spent life on earth usefully? Would Hell operate as a place where the evil are punished? Or is it a fun place for the wicked?

Reading Ravi Gupta's book on a serious issue but looked at in a light-hearted narrative of the functioning of Heaven and Hell and understanding the evolving human mind in a new materialistic value system makes for very interesting reading. It compels us to think of our own lives and how we lead them. It questions our obsession with material things on earth, yet surprisingly it also questions the existence of afterlife and the powers that be. The thoughts are weaved into a story narrative that is easily understood in a world full of corporate warfares. Having spent most of his life in the corporate world it is not surprising that the author uses terminology of the corporate world in an effort to explain his concepts of institutions that we hardly associate with the corporate world. But it does end up making the narrative interesting. Corporate strategies that may work in winning market shares, motivating performance, enhancing productivity, may not work when the perspectives of time and space are changed in celestial abodes. What seems to work in an existing ecosystem may be disastrous when transposed into a different system where the meaning and purpose of life are different. Heaven, Hell and God and the Devil are well used metaphors while tackling issues of good and evil that concern us all. Navigating the after world using corporate structures is an interesting and fresh perspective that the author explores successfully and makes us think of how we should deal with these issues in our own daily lives here on earth. He does take on the jingoism used by misguided community leaders, positioning themselves as divinely ordained to buy legitimacy but are out to promote their own interests. He questions many existing belief systems. You may disagree but you cannot overlook the fact that such questioning should be welcomed. The tongue-in-cheek observations on many issues do make us introspect and that I think is the success of the narrative.

Subhash Ghai
Writer, Director, Producer, Educationist

Prologue

The writer acquires godlike powers as he wields his pen. He could be the lord almighty wielding a magic wand creating characters the way he likes, killing characters that do not suit his narrative, creating a narrative that can wind through the mind of his reader in a cathartic way to manipulate the feelings and emotions of the reader to virtually set aside his rational thinking and make him believe in the mystical world created around him, believe in the powers of the mighty characters, believe in the distinction between right and wrong, and give the reader a feeling of empowerment through the protagonist that his problems can be resolved if and only if the reader believes in the narration.

Interesting, how words, sounds, thoughts, situations created out of nothing, virtually nothing, can occupy the mind space and make a real person believe in the unreal. Believe in the augmented and virtual reality. It is the power of a well-narrated story that compels the mind to think, act or believe in the desired direction. Over a period of time some narrations and stories acquire a life of their own. The pen is indeed mightier than the sword.

Until recently, many of these stories, particularly in civilizations with strong oral traditions, combined with folklore performances through dance, drama, music gave rise to myths and mythologies that grew way beyond the writer or creator's imagination. The multitude of stories as a genre combined over a period of time, intertwined and, even though highly illogical, took on a life of their own as legends, histories, and even religious mythologies with key characters evolving to the status of gods. Gods that soon took on characteristics that could not be challenged as they were by tradition accepted by the people; accepted because that is what was ingrained into them through narration right through their childhood, and challenging them after thousands of years of acceptance was nothing short of blasphemy. Such traditions, mythologies and stories had provided the much needed balm to societies always at war with each other or with other tribes and often provided the light needed in a confused external environment where distinguishing the right from the wrong under differing circumstances had become difficult. The narrations themselves evolved over time to reflect changing values of the society and often established themselves as the gospel truth or law.

Mythology has generally had a far more interesting narratology than history. The patrons of history were often the rulers or the ruling class and history served their needs better by projecting their victories and achievements. It was the ancient world's PR and publicity. History was manipulated to serve the needs of the rulers of the times. Emphasis was shifted in a way that projected the ruler as a victor and where there was defeat this was often interpreted as defeat owing to deceit or adoption of unethical means by the enemy. As opposed to history, mythology served more the interests of the proletariat as there were no limitations on the narrators. This allowed for a far more creative development with the mind set free and the characters that emerged were characters that the proletariat would actually have loved to see as the real rulers.

The evolution of godlike characters created through well meaning narratives by story tellers over a period of time and the acquisition by these characters of super powers including powers to create and operate the universe, to create and control life and even to determine the fate post life are features that need to be studied. Often the unreal gets real and seems more real than the real.

What would indeed be interesting to know is: what if the principal characters in the narrative actually could come alive and had an opportunity to talk about themselves as real characters instead of playing out the characters with powers scripted by the writer or creator? Would they reflect the narrator's narrative or would they give the narration their own twist? Would these characters who had acquired such super powers be willing to shed the powers conferred upon them and acknowledge their frailty? Or would they have been subsumed by what was conferred upon them once upon a time, and now enjoy such powers without limit in their virtual world to the extent that they do not want to give them up in the real world? Would they be just like any dictator who having come to power using divine benediction as a tool to usurp power, now justifies his status in the interest of the good of the people and refuses to surrender power?

The narrator in this novel has randomly selected characters that are largely familiar to readers but the narrative could as easily apply to characters not selected in this narration. The characters are placed in difficult situations that could arise in any rational modern-day situation cornering the principal character into responding to the people until the character finds it necessary to finally come out of the narrative and express his real feelings rather than live the lie of the narrative.

St Peter's Presentation

The gods are assembled in the large central circular hall in Heaven known as the Hall of Thoughts. The Hall, which is a luxurious circular enclosed amphitheatre, is a fusion of classic and modern style of architecture resembling a huge doughnut made of crystal and gold. The ceiling is richly painted and resembles the Sistine Chapel. There are no pillars, no visible doors or windows. There are beautiful virtual curtains in lovely floral designs moving smoothly on thought control determining the intensity of natural light within the Hall. The floral motifs of the curtains look real enough to simulate an ambience of a beautiful garden. The floor is covered with rich Persian-looking carpets with intricate multilayered artworks inspired by legends on earth and other planets.

Comfortable sofas with rich tapestry are laid out spaciously and there are tables made of glass with the table-tops doubling up as interactive screens. The fusion design of the Hall of Thoughts blends with modern communication aides including a large super 4D Real Definition Holographic Digital Cycloramic Screen.

What however draws one's attention is not the beauty of the Hall of Thoughts, its architecture or furnishing, but the assembled gods. They are the icons and religious legends of earth but seen here in flesh and blood. The surrealism of the moment does make one wonder if it is a dream, a reality or an illusion. These are the very gods who the earthlings have been praying to, wanting to see, speak to, touch and seek responses from. They have never been seen on earth. Merely visualized, imagined, written about and venerated. They have dwelt in the minds, in discussions and in places of worship through various artistic forms. So the moment does not feel real. Here the gods seem human. Their physical presence in such a large group seems to both confirm the belief in their existence and the lack of uniqueness and potency that always surrounded them on earth.

The gods are assembled in their lovely robes. This could almost be a fancy dress contest or a fashion show or a costume party if it was on earth. The gods in costumes and apparel accessories are seen engaged in light animated discussions in groups. The conversation seems intellectual with discussions spanning time zones of the past, the present and the future; debates about the living and the non living interspersed with arguments about galaxies and planetary systems. The atmosphere though animated is relaxed and informal, one that is associated with special occasions when families meet after a long interval of time. The gathering of such a plethora of gods does appear to be a rare event even in Heaven.

One can easily identify in the assembly male and female Greek gods, Hindu deities, Sikh gurus, Buddha, Jesus Christ, the Prophet and messengers of God from all faiths and religions. One can also see many faces that look familiar but are not instantly recognizable.

Angels, *farishta*s and *apsara*s are seen in attendance.

God himself, though not seen, appears to be seated at what can be described as the head of the circular doughnut amphitheatre. There appears a soft radiant hypnotic light where God is seated with no well-defined contours.

St Peter glides into the amphitheatre apparently through the glass walls. It is this unobstructed movement that breaks the otherwise seeming reality and raises questions about the reality of the situation. One can sense that this is a different world.

St Peter approaches the crystal podium and requests the assembled to take their seats. As those assembled settle down, St Peter looks towards God as if seeking his approval to commence the proceedings. He seems to receive the approval as he begins the proceedings in all earnestness with his address.

'Respected gods, lords and Almighty,' he begins, 'although we are connected through online thought on a regular basis there is no substitute to a physical assembly together in this beautiful Hall of Thoughts after a fairly long time. I know you have all been preoccupied with your various trans galactic activities, yet we are delighted to have you all here together and I am happy that the omnipotent Almighty has found time from his busy schedules across the universe to attend a meet which for reasons you will appreciate shortly is of utmost importance in deciding the future road map for Heaven. While the information database and analytics reports on all happenings around the universe are available to one and all, the recent report of Heaven's research wing has raised some alarming questions. You will appreciate that it is always difficult to address an assembly of those who already know and can read my mind.

'Yet, the key reason for today's meet is the concern expressed by many of the gods on the report of Heaven's research wing. The report throws up some startling facts.

'One, Heaven is rapidly losing market share of human souls to Hell.

'Two, Heaven is no longer the preferred destination of these souls. In fact, Hell seems to be the first preference of a large number of souls, more particularly the younger ones.

'Three, the changing demographics may affect the delicate balance between Heaven and Hell.

'Let me run you through the details of the research findings and then seek your opinion on how we should be tackling the issues.

'Those of us responsible for the admission of souls to Heaven are in a dilemma over the admission standards. The flow of souls into Heaven has come down to a trickle.

'There are strategic, tactical and operational issues that may need to be reviewed. Until recently we never had to deal with limited soul flow problems. Heaven was always the first choice of souls and our function was limited to choosing the best from among the souls from earth knocking on Heaven's doors.

'There were clearly defined criteria for admission into the portals of Heaven. Over a period of time, value systems seem to have changed on earth. For example, greed is now believed to be good. Evil is good. End results are everything.

'There are also other more fundamental issues. These include the way we should respond to the marketing campaign launched by the Devil and his emissaries.'

St Peter proceeds to make a super HD Holographic 4D PowerPoint presentation. Graphic and visual slides and video holograms appear behind St Peter in thin air as if reading the mind of the speaker without any visible gadget or manual intervention or the presence of any screen. St Peter explains each slide as the statistics presented in some of the slides through graphs and pie charts emphasize that Heaven is becoming less and less attractive to the earthlings and Hell is seemingly getting more attractive.

The 'market share' of souls is demonstrated to have risen significantly in favour of Hell over the previous two decades and continues to be on the rise.

St Peter presents the possible reasons for the demographic shift. The speculated reasons include:

Heaven is being perceived as a boring place to live in.

Heaven is too restrictive in its membership.

The Devil's campaign to market Hell as a fun place is yielding results.

The Devil is certainly able to enter the human mind and influence it through a high intensity marketing campaign with instant gratification leading the mind to believe that Hell is a better place to be in when finally departing earth. The Devil is also encouraging the youngsters to leave the earth early rather than lead a full life on earth. St Peter further points out that the best of talent on earth is being lost to Hell, while sedentary non-achievers, research scholars, scientists and, surprisingly, non-believers are entering Heaven. The age profile of Heaveners is significantly older than that of Hellers. Earthlings obviously seem to be getting disillusioned by Heaven, which is being perceived as a place with a predictable lifestyle and little if any gainful activity. Earthlings are increasingly doubting the very existence of God and feel very let down that their prayers are rarely answered. Often the people who are most religious seem to be suffering the most on earth and the illogic that this is some kind of a god-designed test for the believers is now increasingly being questioned. Theories of evolution are finding acceptance and scientific research and better knowledge of the universe and its origin is leading to open questioning not merely by the scientific community but also by the layman about the very existence of the Almighty. The believers are increasingly expecting that the Lord will make an appearance, as convincing evidence that would demolish the theories being presented by the non-believers and redeem their faith in the Almighty. However there has been no move to make this course correction or rectify the rapidly sliding belief levels. St Peter points out that there may be a faith crisis and erode the brand equity of God and Heaven.

Unfortunately the profile of the believers is increasingly veering towards the fundamentalists who are interpreting religious texts to support killings, genocide and worse, and are promising easy access to Heaven making Heaven look like a large brothel of virgins waiting to serve those who stand by such extremist beliefs that are covertly being spread by the Devil.

The initial relaxed atmosphere in the Hall of Thoughts is seen to be changing and now appears to be getting tense as slide after slide points towards the Devil scoring over Heaven. The implication is that the Devil is scoring over God though any direct reference implying Devil's victory over God is avoided. There is a lot of murmur among the gods and some express doubts about the authenticity and accuracy of the report, quoting the growing numbers of places of worship.

The general belief is that Hell is despised by one and all and people have been working and praying all their lives to find a place in Heaven, the ultimate reward for a fruitful and meaningful afterlife. Everyone wants peace, security, happiness, or so it has been believed. Nobody would like to live in the fires of Hell and be a slave unto Satan.

St Peter reaffirms that the facts and figures are based on research reports of Heaven's R&D cell, and drawn from a study of two decades of data; there is little chance of an error and the error margins arc unlikely to exceed a few per cent points. The general belief is that the facts and figures presented, if true, as St Peter tends to believe, are startling and need to be considered seriously. Hell is certainly offering something that seems more attractive, if not actually better than Heaven. Preliminary findings seem to be that earthlings are no longer seeking a lifestyle that is perceived as boring, sedentary or predictable. Earthlings are preferring the unpredictable, action-packed roller coaster lifestyle of Hell that seems far more adventurous even if hazardous or uncomfortable. Although Heaven offers unlimited peace and joy, the perception in the minds of earthlings about Heaven is different, incorrect and distorted. This impression needs to be rectified. The Devil certainly seems to be an icon that is offering a better brand connectivity among the younger earthlings.

The god of prayers refers to the slides presented by St Peter on the inadequate responses to prayers and the total collapse of a response system. In defense he states that if one is to go by the volume of prayers, it would appear that the awareness and desire to attain Heaven is very high. The prayer quotient and numbers are on the rise. The fact that every day and night over three billion prayers are received is a sign of a strong confidence level in the gods. The god of prayers admits that this still means that about half the adult population is not praying and more needs to be done to reach out to those not praying to get them to reach out to Heaven, and efforts are on to push earthlings to pray using awe and power of natural forces.

The problem is more about dealing with and responding to the prayers. These prayers come in over a hundred languages and in thousands of dialects. They vary in duration from under a minute to over an hour. While most come directly from individuals, many come through group callings led by the so-called ambassadors of Heaven, designated on earth through fancy titles of priest, mullahs, rabbis, pundits, gurus and their hierarchies. There is a major problem of sorting out all the prayers, categorizing them, analyzing them, comprehending them and responding to them. Most of the prayers relate to people wanting wealth, more wealth and generally getting rich overnight. The concept of wealth on earth is not the valuable, but the tangible that can be monetized. Earthlings fail to understand that Heaven does not have a monetary or a banking system nor offers financial services. Heaven is not a Federal bank printing currency, nor a Western Union running a money transfer service. One can only help those who help themselves. Heaven adds enlightenment, wealth and value to people's lives, not money into their bank accounts. Heaven can only show people the right direction.

Unfortunately people do not want to help themselves. They see only what they want to see and hear only what they want to hear. So the voice of reason and the light of guidance are lost to them. Although Heaven responds to the prayers by providing people guidance, the same is unheeded and interpreted as absence of Heavenly response.

The god of prayers further adds that there are other practical issues. Many prayers seek to hurt or harm others. Heaven cannot respond meaningfully to these. There is reason to believe that there are techniques deployed by the Devil to overload and sabotage Heaven's response systems. Religious leaders influenced by the Devil promise the unsuspecting an abode in Heaven with virgins-in-waiting in exchange for killing those not following the religious leaders, even if they are loyal to God. Thus the importance of the religious leaders is greater than that of God on earth. Since the religious leaders are present in flesh and blood and promise instant gratification they tend to build up better credibility and hence the policy of non-appearance in person needs to be reviewed. The messengers have in effect become the message.

The earthlings want health and happiness but do everything that will ensure poor health and depression. Health cannot be distributed. Earthlings need to work on their body and mind, be disciplined and earn their health.

The youngsters pray only during an earth ritual called 'exams' and seek good grades when they have not studied and have been partying all year round.

'Now how do I deal with all these requests?' questions the god of prayers.

'As per policy guidelines we can only answer prayers in those cases where intangibles are requested and where people have shown genuine desire to help themselves or others and not just depend on largesse falling into their laps,' he adds.

He further goes on to say, 'We need to change things at the origination end and not focus on further improving our response mechanism. We are only getting garbage in the name of prayers. As they say in computer parlance, garbage in, garbage out. I would urge that we revise the norms at origination, bringing about a greater awareness that Heaven is not into fulfilling material needs. Wealth and happiness are not functions of material accumulation and artificially created monetization mechanism. Health and peace are an internal mind function, not an externally induced well-being phenomenon.'

There is discussion on the issues raised with pertinent, interesting and thought-provoking interventions. The arguments are primarily around the purpose of Heaven, the philosophy of a higher mind space and the goals proposed to be achieved. The issue of the very purpose of Heaven is questioned. Maybe a solution could be that all souls are just allowed to wander in the universe for eternity rather than being divided between Heaven and Hell. Maybe the soul is extinguished along with death. Maybe this will put an end to the undeclared war between Heaven and Hell.

Questions are raised if Heaven should lower its thought processes and align these along earthly lines where value measurements are different, where success is linked to financial results.

It is pointed out that efforts to raise the values of earthlings by sending gods to earth from time to time in various avatars has failed. Each step forward has ultimately been reversed by self-appointed preachers, resulting in two steps backwards.

The quality of discussion is of a high order and the debate is very enlightening on a varied range of issues. There is a lot of introspection on Heaven's own beliefs in the perception of the human mind and the willingness to change these. The plethora of suggestions also makes it difficult to decide on a line of action. Some of the issues raised are questioned and the problems posed are put into varied perspectives. There is no screaming, shouting or denouncing. Interestingly, even the success of the Devil is praised and 'Give the Devil his due' is a thought expressed.

Everyone looks towards God, knowing that he should have all the answers. God has been just too busy in his experimentation with the creation of new universes and galaxies, studying new forms of life while presuming that all is well in Heaven and the gods in-charge would have taken good care of the older institutions like Heaven and earth. God himself seems unperturbed with the presentation of St Peter.

God finally speaks but prefers to explain some of his new experiments in far away galaxies. He indicates that a lot of correction and direction in his new experimentation in far away galaxies has come from the shortcomings of life on earth and from the wonderful work being done by thinkers, scientists and scholars in Heaven. He however needs to see the results of his new experiments, which will be known only over evolutionary periods. He confesses that he has been somewhat disappointed with the way the human model has shaped up—not quite what he had intended. He notes that human beings have evolved to be too selfish, ungrateful, insecure and violent for his own liking and are significantly deviating from what the survival instinct should have thrown up or what the survival of the fittest should have achieved. It wasn't what he had intended through evolution. However, being a firm believer in not interfering with the laws of nature, or of evolution, and being of the firm view that freedom of thought, speech and action, should be allowed to earthlings to evolve and grow as they deem appropriate, he has refused to interfere. God clarifies that he never intended creating a world of his desire. He intended that the world should create itself through an evolutionary process that followed basic scientific and natural principles. Any intervention by him would be against the spirit of evolution and natural scientific laws. Intervention would be seen as miracles and these would be undesirable deviations and a distortion. Despite his strictly non-interventionist policy there appears to be no dearth of human assumptions of his intervention by way of miracles as if that is what was necessary to establish his own existence.

Contrary to the earthlings' belief that God is controlling every move and movement, action and reaction on earth and in Heaven, God states that he had been confident that the laws of physics, evolution, and the instinct for survival would result in an organic, dynamic yet harmonious world. The human species, however, having overcome the barriers of basic survival, and having moved to higher capabilities of thought and questioning, was now also able to control to a fair extent its own future development. The understanding of the science behind creation and life had certainly enabled the human species to be proactive in DNA engineering, cloning, mutation, morphing or modifying. Processes, which took evolution millions of years to perfect after many trials and errors, were now being put in place without long-term trials or the understanding of long-term implications. This could lead to catastrophic results if the technologies developed were either misused or inadequately understood.

God admits that he had not counted on the overindulgence of earthlings in physical pleasures, nor on the Devil's intervention through unfair means to fuel thoughts that would derail the plans for harmony. He had also not foreseen mankind's most devastating invention—money. Monetization of commodities, goods and services reflected in the common denominator understood as money has fuelled greed, violence, power battles and all things perceived as evil. He was monitoring the various new life forms he had created and was constantly studying their evolution to discover the elements and ecosystems that are leading to the most evolved forms of life.

God confesses that he only helped put the right ingredients in place and allowed the laws of nature, the laws of physics and chemistry, the laws of nano particles that he designed as the basic structure to operate over time to evolve into more meaningful life. The trigger for the more evolved Homo sapiens was really the networking of the nerves that allowed understanding and grasp of logic, of relating images with sound, of recording knowledge in signs and symbols in transmittable form. He had only been a catalyst to creation, not the creator himself, and he can only take credit for creating the laws of nature that ensured creation. He states that the earthlings' conception of Him creating life and people overnight through a wand is very simplistic, naïve and totally incorrect. Yes, his powers as an embodiment of Nature itself allow him to play and intervene in the processes, but the right approach is to allow the laws of nature to determine how events would unfold. He should only be focusing on the laws themselves and not on the events. That is what he has attempted in other galaxies. God speaks about how evolution in other parts of the universes have led to far more meaningful forms of life which have attained far greater heights in form, content and style.

Referring to the immediate problem at hand, God asks for suggestions. The Council of Gods comes up with many. Among these, Lord Shankara suggests declaration of war on Hell; Naradmooni, the wily broker, suggests sabotage of Devil's plans through a covert operation; ban money, suggests Jesus; adopt an aggressive marketing campaign, suggests a Greek god; structurally modify the human mind, suggests the Prophet.

God says these are not suggestions that would be justifiable by the touchstone of Heaven's Best Practices. The problem, he says, is that they are thinking short term. Ends do not justify means. Using whatever means to achieve an end is the Devil's philosophy, and under pressure to outdo the Devil, principles should not be compromised. 'How would we be different from the Devil if we resorted to unfair means like the Devil,' asks God. God emphasizes the need to ensure Best Practices and Heavenly governance of the highest standards. Various gods have in fact been preaching these principles during their visits to earth, and while the principles have been appreciated by the earthlings to be fundamentally sound, the teachings themselves have been distorted by the self-proclaimed guardians of religion to their own advantage by claiming proximity to the Divine. This empowerment has led to power centres and resultant conflicts among the religious power centres—conflicts that are fought through the unsuspecting common man.

God emphasizes that mankind has introduced money as an easy measurable commodity. Money's success lies in the fact that it is an easily measurable unit that can be associated with all tangible goods and services. Earthlings are apparently happy with valuing what is measurable instead of measuring what is valuable.

God says, 'In Heaven we measure what is valuable, we measure honesty, fidelity, sacrifice, commitment, knowledge, wisdom, integrity, friendship, trust among other invaluables. Earthlings are unable to measure these values. So they value the more measurable things such as land, buildings, metals, possessions, stones, etc., which are all derived from the earth, with their value depending on the supply and demand and manipulations thereof. Every tangible article, including human beings and their parts, has a valuation, a price tag. It's easy to understand the price tag and to place the item in context and in relation to cost of other items. It clarifies where each item stands in a hierarchy defining each one's place or slot in life.

Either you change the price tag adopting whatever skills and power you can command or you get into the slot determined by your price tag. In Heaven we have no money and monetization. Hence there is no place for price tags. This leads to a level of equality that the earthlings may find hard to comprehend. The system makes it more difficult for administrators used to working with monetary policies to determine performances, output, productivity, incentives, motivation, etc. Values on earth are so very different from those in Heaven. Who, for example, would price stones that are made of nothing but carbon that earthlings call diamonds at such ridiculously high prices? Merely because there is a short supply of these stones on earth and they refract light, a demand is created through marketing strategies, and an item that is in abundance in other planets and galaxies becomes a valuable commodity on earth. The value is really in the light source and in the eye that receives the light source, not in the stone that refracts it; but the human mind is yet to understand where the real value lies.

'Monetization may not have been a bad system had it not been used for the wrong purpose. When an earthling comes to Heaven we do not permit him to bring any of the monetizable commodities with him. We do not measure his worth by how much money he accumulated; we measure the invaluables, the intangibles that come with him. Maybe we should evolve a system whereby the invaluables can be denominated in measurable quantities. But perhaps they would then no longer be invaluables.'

God indicates that he is not worried about the declining market share of souls. He emphasizes that Heaven needs to continue to build its Brand. Branding must not be confused with advertising; the two may be linked but advertising is about hawking a product, promoting its tangible values like price, technical or quality specifications, service and guarantees, performance expectations, etc., while Brand emphasizes values and consumer experience, the consumer's desire to be linked with the product, to take pride in owning or using it, to recommend it.

Finally, one of the gods meekly asks why God, who knows everything, needs suggestions from the Council. God responds that the interventionist way of putting things right in a jiffy is contrary to the laws of nature. And the way he wants is not the way it needs to be or should be. The right way is that the living are engaged in their evolution. His original design envisaged the living and the non living, with the living having liberty to contribute and work their way to determining their own destinies within the overall laws of nature. Either this basic structure needs to be discarded or the laws laid down need to be changed. He himself does not favour a solution that would dilute the self-determining powers of the living and push them more towards characteristics of the non living. Of course, the problem is that more the liberty provided by higher intelligence, greater the chances of its misuse; yet taking that liberty away would be a treatment worse than the ailment.

One of the gods asks why God created Devil in the first place. He should never have done that. Can the Devil not be destroyed by God to end all problems?

God says, 'It would be very dangerous not to have someone demonstrating to you where you are going wrong. The idea was never to create Devil as an Evil. Devil was essentially meant to be like a competitor so as to ensure continuous improvements. However the Devil is resorting to unfair means and instead of healthy competition leading to improved quality for all living creatures, we have ended up with the Devil wanting to destroy his own creator and has even entered into a pact with the earthlings, offering them cheap, pleasure-enhancing thrills in lieu of their souls.'

'I do not know how we could go about rectifying this situation,' laments St Peter. 'Shall we seek advice from this Council, or commission a research to understand their needs and find solutions?'

'Our own researchers will not be able to understand the changing human mind. An appropriate earth-based consultant or consultancy firm that can examine all the issues may be a better starting point,' suggests the god of prayer.

'It's only the earthlings who can best understand the changing needs and perceptions of their likes and dislikes. We may be wrong in our presumptions. So let us get a researched report from an earth-based consultancy before we tinker with any solutions. Let them spell out what they want and let us discuss thereafter based on the findings.'

Jesus affirms the suggestion and states that a consultant be appointed to come up with the reasons for the changes in human thought process, the measures to remedy the same, recommendations on marketing administration of and responses to prayers, checkmating the Devil, and beating the Hell out of competition…and…the competition from Hell.

God nods in approval arguing that using his powers to destroy Devil will be like throwing out the baby with the bathwater.

'Never before have so many powerful entities been assembled in one place,' He notes. 'We could use our power to create, to destroy or to change the world. Or we can decide not to use the power and let the change happen through self-actualization, evolution or the play of natural forces.

'If unfettered powers are used there is the danger that the same may be misused. After all, the concept of Right is known only because we know what is Wrong.'

All the gods nod their approval.

'The Devil certainly is doing the thing right, even though he is not doing the right thing. It was my intention to create, or rather to encourage evolution in a direction that leads to a species that can think, a species that can make its own choices, that can differentiate between right and wrong. St Peters' presentation is a good reminder that the species is making its choices and getting more assertive. It is our view in this Council that the species is not choosing correctly and prefers to embrace the Devil. From the Devil's perspective the species is choosing correctly. We do have the option of reducing the entry barrier in Heaven, sending a new Prophet down to earth to influence humans or to understand the issue influencing the decision of the species.'

God further adds, 'I am inclined to accept the suggestion made that we need to understand the human mind better, find out how it is being influenced and analyze the factors that are contributing to the process of decision making. The human mind has changed significantly and we seem to be at a loss to understand the changes. Even if I do understand the evolving human mind, it is only fair to get an opinion from human experts, consultants, for only another human mind would be able to comprehend and analyze the changing dynamics and give us the inputs needed to help take the right decision. Let us reassemble to discuss the consultant's report once received to study the feasibility of implementation.'

As the all knowing, God hints that he can anticipate the answers and is aware of the right decision needed to be taken, but he would rather that the decisions evolve through a process of understanding and research involving all stakeholders. A unilateral decision would be against the Best Practices and universal scientology that is responsible for the working of the universe.

St Peter is directed to take care of getting the consultant's report early.

'Yes, my Lord,' says St Peter. He is not too happy about God's repeated reference to evolution and under playing creation. He cannot hide his disappointment that God has not opted to just terminate the Devil despite overwhelming evidence of wrong doings, but refrains from any expression knowing that his views may already have been mind read by God.

He assures all assembled that further information would be communicated through @Thought from time to time and thanks everyone for having graced the occasion.

St Paul proposes the formal vote of thanks and invites the gods to join the dinner service.

God disappears as the rest of the assembly is seen in animated conversation while enjoying the drinks and food.

***

The Appointment of Consultants

A Hoogle search of reputed consultants on earth throws up many names. St Peter after some due diligence shortlists two.

R&D are among the most reputed consultants dealing with the biggest companies globally. They have a strong international reputation and have offices in all major cities around the world. R&D is headquartered in New York and its chairman is Donald Duven, son of the founder-promoter of the company who has recently taken over from his father, the senior Duven. Donald apart from being a very shrewd businessman is an avid golfer. The only drawback is that he is a highly irreligious person.

ABC are a leading global consultancy firm headquartered in London. They have in the previous two years done M&A deals close to a trillion dollars. They have a list of clients that includes the Fortune 100 Companies and do not normally undertake consultancies for companies that are not listed in the Fortune 500 roll of honour. Their stock is at an all-time high with a PE ratio indicating great confidence in their future earnings potential. There is wide acclaim of their reach and prowess in M&A deals despite the fact that their last M&A deal merging two of the top Fortune 50 Companies resulted in massive loss in shareholder value post the merger.

The loss was never assigned to the consultancy firm for having put together wrong bedmates, but was assigned to bad post-merger management.

Jason, the chairman of the group, is a very gregarious person with a flamboyant lifestyle. He is known to love a celebrity lifestyle and spends a lot of time in the US, throwing lavish parties and mixing with Hollywood actresses and models. He is however a very religious person on Sundays. It is his way of buying peace with God for the sins of the week. He runs several charities primarily focused on healthcare and sanitation in Africa where he is also consultant in his personal capacity for some of the leading dictatorial regimes in arms acquisition and mining.

St Peter would like to choose the religious Jason over the non-believer Donald Duven as consultant.

God suggests he choose R&D as Donald is more likely to give independent views being a non-believer. R&D is targeted by a reluctant St Peter as consultants for restructuring Heaven, but he now must get them to consent.

St Peter steps into a huge skyscraper near Times Square known as the Vampire Estate Building. It now is the tallest building in the world. As he walks through the security checks, a tall, stout guard looks at him with suspicion. The security guard manning the scanning machine seems momentarily confused. He has not seen this guy in white cassock on the monitor. He wants to stop him but changes his mind as there is a long queue, it being a Monday morning and the pressure on rapidly clearing people for work is high. He also reasons that he may have made a mistake, for no one can go past without an X-ray image appearing on the screen. St Peter hurries past the guard and moves towards the high-speed lifts. He steps out on the 113th floor and walks towards an impressive glass door that says R&D Consultants. This is the reception floor of the fifty-year-old reputed consultancy firm that owns several floors of the skyscraper.

'Sir, can I be of help?' asks the office secretary, a pretty, well-dressed, well-manicured, well-groomed young lady.

'I am Peter. Saint Peter if you please. We have done a Hoogle search and shortlisted your company as one that could provide consultancy services that we are looking for.'

'You mean Google, sir. What kind of services are you seeking, sir?'

'No, not Google. Google is the earth version and I don't mean Google earth. In Heaven we have the Hoogle, which is not Google's Heaven version. We do have a Hoogle Earth though that tells us all about matters on earth. Problem is it does not tell us all that we need to know which is why I am here. Hopefully you may be able to provide the answers.'

St Peter presents his visiting card that just says 'St Peter, Heaven Inc', with an email ID Peter@pearlygates.hvn. The card is made of gold.

The secretary has dealt with all kinds of clients but this one seems very quirky. Seeing the card made of gold, she cannot just dismiss this client. That's what she would normally have done with a potential client arriving without a prior appointment.

'Sir, I am sorry but can we come to the point? What exactly are you seeking and what company do you represent as we do not undertake consultancy for companies other than Fortune 500 Companies.'

'I represent what you would call Heaven Inc. We are not a Fortune 500 Company, but we control the fortunes of those controlling Fortune 500 Companies.'

'Sir, do you have an appointment, or are you seeking one?'

'No, I do not have an appointment. But I know that both Ronald and Donald are in their office and they would be quite pleased for me to anoint them, if you set up the appointment, of course. I will be offering a large consultancy. Just go ahead and ask them.'

'Sir, please take a seat. I shall see if either of them can meet with you without a prior appointment. You will appreciate that they are both very busy people. I will see if I can set up a meeting with one of our business development managers.'

'Thank you. But I would much rather meet Ronald or Donald since they would be the decision makers.'

The secretary connects with Ronald. 'There's this guy who has come in without a reference. He is talking of a large consultancy assignment. But it's not from a Fortune 500 Company. Would you like to meet him? He looks respectable but—' and she softens her tone as she adds, 'he is queer. Flaunts a visiting card made of gold.'

'I have seen enough queer people in this business,' says Ronald. 'Quirkiness is a sign of success it seems. It's the colour of money that matters and believe me there are many of these guys who do not run listed companies yet have higher net worth than Fortune 500 Companies. Yes, I will see him in a minute. Never let an opportunity go by without evaluating.'

As the secretary escorts St Peter to the conference room and seats him, she fills him in on some recent achievements of R&D including the 175 billion dollar merger deal between Macrosoft and Pathway.

'Would you care for some tea or coffee or maybe some juice?' asks the secretary.

'No, thank you, Vanessa,' says St Peter.

Vanessa exits wondering how the gentleman knew her name. At work she is only known as Ms Fernandez.

As St Peter waits he looks around and sees the vision statement of R&D. It's an impressive call to action addressed to its executives with slogans about the client being the centre of the business. It also speaks about their 23000-strong global team and its commitment to excellence.

'Good morning, Ronald.'

'Mr Peter I presume.'

'Yes, you may call me Peter. These days titles are no longer fashionable.'

'Can I offer you some coffee?'

'No, thanks. I'll skip the coffee.'

'You guessed right. I am Ronald, CEO of R&D,' says Ronald handing his visiting card with both hands and a slight bow.

'Bless you my child.'

Ronald is not very comfortable being referred to as child, nor with the patronizing attitude of St Peter. He however controls himself and gestures to St Peter to take a seat and sits down himself. He asks if St Peter would like to spell out his problem.

St Peter tells him briefly that they are looking for a consultancy to review the way they are operating and to find ways and means of ensuring that they improve their operations and market share.

'Thank you for considering us, but the company you represent—is it an American company? It's not in the Forbes list nor a Fortune 500 Company.'

'Oh it's very valuable,' says St Peter.

'You mean it's an unlisted high value company? We generally only deal with Fortune 500 Companies.'

'Your fortunes could multiply.'

'What does the company deal in?'

'In souls.'

'Soles? As in shoe soles?'

'No. As in afterlife.'

'Are you undertakers?'

'No, we take over from the undertaker.'

'I'm confused. We…'

'I see that. You needn't be. We are proposing a restructuring to increase our market share.'

'Who are your competitors?'

'Well. Hell.'

'Hell who?'

'Hell.'

'I am sorry, I don't understand. I don't know if you are using Heaven as a kind of metaphor. From what I gather you want a very comprehensive consultancy job from us. As you may be aware, we are expensive and believe in advance payment,' says Ronald hoping to dissuade St Peter from proceeding with the assignment. And such an assignment could involve hundreds of millions of dollars. A million dollars just to prepare a brief, time frames and costs.

'We could pay you in kind. In kindness, that is. We could ease your move to Heaven and you may perhaps be assured of a place there. A place in the sun so to say.'

'Sir, I think you may be at the wrong place. We do not take on consultancies without reference and our fees are a minimum of ten million dollars.'

'Oh, would God's reference do? We can add a lot more value than dollars. We don't deal with tangibles.'

'Don't you have a reference of someone well known?'

'You mean better known than God?'

'Can you pay upfront?' asks Ronald, fully convinced that Peter is either crazy or eccentric.

'No. We could pay you in more valuable terms.'

'Sir, can we get a reference from your bankers.'

'In Heaven there are hardly any bankers. Matter of fact there are no banks. Nor money. So we don't really need banks. We operate on trust. In God we trust.'

'We would not take up this assignment without a due diligence. You understand you are not a listed company and Federal regulations require us to know our clients.'

'Sure, you can do due diligence.'

'We would like to send one of our senior executives to your company headquarters if you pay a million dollars as set-up costs.'

'Sure, anytime. We will have him picked up. We do not do return delivery though.'

'Why not?'

'Do you know of anyone who has returned from Heaven?'

'You mean Heaven as in "up there"?' says Ronald pointing upwards.

'Yes, up there. But it could be down as well. The universe has no up or down, these directions are your orientation; now if you are happy with Heaven being up then it's up. It's a lovely place, I assure you. No one who's been there wants to come back in any case.'

'Well…er…I will have to check up.

'Sir, we shall do a company search and then get back to you with our proposal if we are satisfied about your credentials.'

'Well, if you are not interested, maybe I should approach ABC Consultants. Meet Jason, I suppose.'

Ronald looks disconcerted. St Peter has struck the right chord. The mention of ABC is a red rag to Ronald. He cannot let Peter go meet Jason. Perhaps the problem posed by St Peter is indeed true. Maybe he is from the Church. Maybe from the Vatican. After all, the Church and Vatican are loaded with assets, with money and donations. Those huge trusts and foundations the Vatican controls invest hundreds of billions of dollars in equity markets—maybe he has access to them. Perhaps he should deal with this more carefully. This guy could be the ticket to big bucks. Ronald remembers the time he had to deal with an Arab. The Arab was an uncouth guy. He almost threw the Arab out of his office. It turned out the Arab was one of the wealthiest guys in the world. He later ended up being at the beck and call of the Arab much against his own wishes, but he had no choice. Donald considered the Arab a premium client. Could this Peter guy be someone similar?

'What, sir, is the nature of the consultancy you are seeking?' asks Ronald somewhat mildly.

'We need to know why people want to go to Hell when there is a better choice in Heaven. Can you find that out for us? Research and tell us what we need to do to make Heaven more attractive. After all that I have seen from the consultancies you have undertaken, it is clear that you have added significant value to your client's results, by way of market share, profitability, profits, PE ratios, share prices, etc. I see your claims all over in WSJ interviews.'

'Yes, we have done reasonably well. We do have a very strong team of analysts. Our Analytics and Business Processes Teams are highly experienced with a vast array of knowledge partners and domain experts who put together well-thought-out solutions for any problem. That, if I may add, is our core strength.

'Your problem does seem to be interesting and challenging,' mutters Ronald. He pretends that he finds the challenge exciting enough. Although he is unsure of where this is leading. He imagines the response of their business rivals when they learn of a contract R&D has bagged with an extraterrestrial entity. He now is determined to go ahead with this assignment if the money is forthcoming. They could in future claim to be the first company to operate beyond the earth.

He is unsure though if any of his executives would be willing to go to Heaven for an assessment, if safe return to earth is not guaranteed.

'Sir, this is getting complicated. We...er...don't work without a monetary consideration. Sir, we don't mean to be rude, but our hands are full at the moment though we could consider assigning resources if the payment is right.'

'Here's my card.' St Peter hands him a card made of pure gold.

Seeing the gold card Ronald changes his mind and adds, 'Of course, we look forward to working with you. I will ask Vanessa to send you our bank details and an invoice for transfer of funds on account of intent to engage, so we know you mean business. You will also need to sign a NDA, I mean a non-disclosure agreement, before we can proceed, plus give us information about your company to satisfy Federal documentation needs. A full form agreement will follow.'

'Money is not what you should be seeking. I could offer you more valuable things. But if money is what you desire, so be it. It's what we are hoping we would change, this mindset about money. And do make surc your bank is not of one those that might declare bankruptcy any day.'

'Thank you, Sir, for your visit.'

St Peter leaves with a 'God Bless You' and greets Vanessa on the way out.

Ronald looks confused but pulls himself together. He is not sure if it was all a dream or just a hoax. Nervously and without speaking a word he gets back to work.

As Ronald sits down in front of his laptop, he picks up the hotline that connects him to his chairman, Donald.

'Donald, you won't believe this but there was this guy claiming to be Peter or St Peter and he wants us to take on a consultancy work for Heaven. He wants us to research on why Heaven is losing its market share of souls to Hell and recommend to them measures to regain market control.'

'That's interesting,' interjects Donald.

'It would be, but this guy seems to be either a fraud or a rich eccentric heir. I am hoping he represents the Vatican. They are loaded with funds and are spending it all in the wrong places. There is hardly any audit of their funds so if you get a toehold to do business with the Vatican that can be reason to pop the champagne in the name of the pope. His visiting card is made of gold. Maybe gold plated—I must verify. Do you think I should report to security? He must be on his way out. Tall, in white robes, and even had the temerity to offer transfer of funds.'

'Sure, do that,' says Donald, 'you never know what this guy may be upto.'

'Yes, I did pack him off, but he said he would transfer funds as an advance. Even took our bank details. Oh my God! Do you think he may be a hacker who may hack into our account? Heck. Maybe it's another one of those Nigerian frauds that offer enormous sums of moneys that don't exist. Let me call security.'

He puts down the phone and immediately connects to security.

'Security, its Ronald, from the 113th floor. There is this guy, looks like a priest, he is in white cassock, if you see him down at security will you…Oh my God…'

Ronald suddenly sees on his iPhone a confirmation mail from his bank of funds transferred from Heaven Inc. He freezes. It's a million dollars! He looks at his laptop. There is another mail from St Peter. Ronald freezes.

'Yes, Mr Ronald. Mr Ronald are you there? Mr Ronald, is everything OK…' repeats security louder each time.

'Oh yes, I mean no. No, it's nothing,' replies Ronald.

'But you screamed "Oh my God." Is everything OK?'

'Yes, yes. I was just er remembering...God...I mean God was remembering me...I mean...sorry.'

He cuts off the phone and calls back Donald.

'Donald, I think you must meet this guy. I don't know which country he is from. He says he's not from earth but does business on earth that touches every soul.'

'Now why on earth would I want to meet someone who is not from earth, Ronald? I thought you were reporting the matter to security. Isn't he some kind of a cyber fraudster? Hope you have alerted the bank.'

'No, no, no! He has actually transferred money into our account. A million dollars! Without any questions, without even a document signed. I think we should definitely do business with him.'

He reads out the mail to Donald.

Ronald, it was a pleasure meeting with you. The money you desire has been transferred into your account. I don't know why you guys so value money. There are far more valuable things in life you may like to look at. Count your blessings, not money. Anyway have the docket ready by next week. God Bless You. Peter.

'Make sure there are no issues of money laundering here, Ronald. We don't want any problems with the Feds with all these new anti-money laundering laws in place.'

Ronald and Donald decide to keep the assignment and contract confidential. Ronald calls up the bank to verify the authenticity of the transfer. The bank confirms the credit transfer but is unable to confirm details of the transferring party beyond stating that it is from a company named Heaven Inc. and a bank called LAXMI. The banker, of Indian origin, says he will check up further details and get back but states that *Laxmi* in the Indian language means wealth and is also the name of the goddess of wealth.

Ronald directs Vanessa to prepare the necessary documentation. He also shoots off a mail to St Peter thanking him for the transfer of funds and letting him know that their lawyers would get in touch with him on the NDA. He states that Vanessa will inform him about the Federal Compliance Documentation needed.

A meeting of key executives who would be involved in the preparation of the brief is called later that day and Ronald explains:

'We are taking on an assignment for a charity foundation that would like to spread the teachings of God on earth in a way that is better understood by people. Not necessarily the religious route. We are not rewriting the Bible, Koran, Geeta or any other holy scriptures. But we need to spread the message of the Lord. Not through the traditional preachy route. We need to think out of the box. We need to make religion sound hep and acceptable to the youth. Maybe through rap music, dance, or whatever. We need to market Heaven. We need to make Heaven a desirable product. The first choice post death. We need to understand our TG and what modes of communication would best work for the TG, what creatives would connect, and what should be the message we deliver. We also need a feedback mechanism on what is working.'

Everyone in the room has a confused look. Before anyone can raise any questions Ronald continues.

'Suppose we were dealing with a company that was into enticing people to die, promising a better life—how would we market their business proposition?'

'Sir,' offers Keith, the chief accounts executive, 'I don't think we should take on such an assignment. Nobody wants to die. What the hell, even if I were offered the best in heaven I wouldn't go nowhere. Not for love. Not for money. Earth is a great place to live in, and Hell may not be a bad option either. In fact, last night I was at this discotheque called Hell—wow that's the place to be in.'

'Keith, we are into providing consultancies. We don't care what business the client is into. We don't care whether the client is doing the right thing or in the right product line. We gotta tell him how to sell their product even if its unmarketable. So let's just focus on that, and I would appreciate if you all focus on the assignment and not respond to chats on your cells during meetings.'

Ronald explains at length the mandate and asks his team to get back with specific focus areas, research approach and modality, Target Groups, time frames, resource requirements, sample audit, and out-of-pocket costs, demographic and geographic dispersals, religious group segmentation, gender differentiation, etc. He indicates that this may be their year's biggest assignment. It may be linked to the Vatican and the client may just be fronting for the Pope. The proposal needs to be prepared soon and a presentation would be made to the client certainly by early next week.

'We may have to work over the weekend. But if we are able to bag the contract you will all get a hefty bonus and remember that whatever be your religious inclination, this project takes precedence,' he adds.

The executives look stunned at the nature and urgency of the assignment, the undisclosed mysterious client, and his financial capability and motives.

All through the week the executives are working round the clock. Connecting with their counterparts and segment experts, going through thousands of existing documents on the subject, searching on Google, researching and putting data and reports together.

After several rounds of internal discussions and notes prepared by various departments, Keith puts together a consolidated report for Ronald. Ronald discusses the report at length with Donald, expressing concern at several issues and pointing out loose ends in the offer for consultancy document. Donald suggests some practical approaches to resolve the issues.

Ronald is in his office going through the draft proposal prepared by Keith and his team. He makes several corrections based on his own research conducted over the previous week and inputs provided by Donald. He finally picks up his intercom, presses some numbers inattentively, as if by habit, and without any effort or thought speaks into the intercom speaker, 'Vanessa, do you have a contact number for this guy calling himself Peter or whatever from Heaven Inc. His card carries no contact number, just an email ID.'

'No, I am afraid, when I asked him he just said he would contact us. But his email ID is there on his card. I Googled and there are over 500 million links against Heaven and St Peter. They must be really popular. You really think this guy is from Heaven? I mean can he really be *the* Saint Peter? You think he may be upset with me for the way I treated him? You know, not bowing down to him. I didn't even offer him a drink. God, what if I end up in Heaven! I am so worried now that he may have read my thoughts. You know, I was debating with Shirley that Hell may be a better place.'

'Oh, I really don't know or care. He certainly is rich. Look at his gold card. Real gold. I had it checked out. He could be linked to some Middle-East ruling family. Oil wealth or plunder, that's where their riches come from. They are the only ones who distribute visiting cards made of gold. Heaven! Fuck. That's all bullshit. Chances are that the client wants to subvert the teachings of the Bible and this is one big conspiracy to push their ideologies through sabotage. I only hope we are not being used in the process and no fundamentalist organization is involved. Anyway, who cares? Donald may even like it. He is probably a non-believer. But if this Peter guy is a Catholic he is probably working for the Church. They are the only ones who can come up with such crazy ideas. Maybe they want to rewrite a Bible more acceptable to the new generation and need inputs for the same. Who cares? It's the money that matters. Let them just pay up, take the report and scoot. I don't believe any of that saint stuff and I don't have the time to find out more about this guy, but I will if they really sign on the deal. Now let me send him a mail and play ball with his game whatever the game is. But yes, next time he is here, treat him royally. Not as Saint Peter but as Sheikh Peter. He is more likely to be an Arab working for some Sheikh.'

Late that night, after many drafts and redrafts Ronald is finalizing a mail to St Peter. He wants to be correct with every word. He can't afford to goof up through any offensive word, yet he needs to protect himself from any potential fraud or money laundering and ensure that the financial interests of the company are adequately protected. He has already discussed the draft with the lawyers and taken their inputs over the week. His final draft reads:

To:
Saint Peter
Heaven Inc

Dear St Peter,

Thank you for your visit to our office last week. I am sorry for a somewhat delayed response but we had to do adequate background work before sending you a meaningful proposal. Your brief, you will appreciate, is unique and we ourselves have not earlier dealt with unlisted and unstructured companies, nor have we worked on a project of a nature defined by you. Yet we consider it a challenge and I am confident of the delivery capabilities of our team. The below proposal is an interim one and may undergo further changes depending on additional detailed inputs and directions we may receive from you.

We confirm receipt of USD one million into our account. We are awaiting your company's details including tax numbers.

We have examined your needs internally and shall present you details of the mandate being undertaken by next week. I am however sending you herewith an indicative cost structure on the proposed consultancy given the wide range, complexity, low acceptable delta for error margins, large geographical dispersal, and the urgency of the task.

This is to confirm that we are prepared to undertake the consultancy subject to the following broad conditions.

1. *We will undertake a detailed study and on-ground research and provide you with consultancies including follow-up execution in agreed areas of*

   a) Crystallizing the issues involved, the problem being faced and the external business environment.

   b) Preparing a road map for the administration, marketing and structuring of Heaven along with a SWOT analysis of Heaven as well as its competitor Hell.

   c) A comparative understanding and recommendations of improving systems, operations, sourcing, placing and training of key executives to enhance efficiencies, coordination and effectiveness of company operations.

   d) Research on earth to understand the human mind, its needs and aspirations post death and the convergence and congruence between the needs/desires of the soul and the services provided in Heaven. The research would cover at least 40k respondents covering all major nations, continents, religious groups, age groups, genders, economic classes. It is clarified that no primary research will be carried out in any location beyond the earth and we will depend on inputs provided by you to us to analyze, draw conclusions and make recommendations on extra-terrestrial locations.

e) The strategies and approach to counter Hell's approach in the marketplace will be recommended and where requested we will engage in its implementation.

f) Involvement in identifying key resources, personnel and agencies to implement the recommendations, post their approval by you.

g) The consultancy duration will be one year. Any delay or extension owing to reasons not of our doing will be chargeable in addition as per our standard hourly rates for such consultancies.

2. *The contract value will be $40,347,450 million (USD forty million three hundred and forty seven thousand four hundred and fifty only) as per details attached. VAT at applicable rates will additionally be payable. This value does not include the implementation phase for which a separate quote will be made once the client clarifies the recommendations it accepts and wants us to implement.*

   You will sign off the exclusive consultancy mandate along with 25% advance payment with the balance payable on pre-specified milestone related dates.

3. *You will sign off the indemnity bond and the confidentiality agreement, as will be notified by our lawyers. You will also sign the full form agreement prior to the commencement of the mandate.*

4. *You will be required to pay additionally all reasonable out of pocket advance for outstation travel, stay at quality hotels,*

printing, etc. We will not be required to seek prior approval for such travels but would submit supporting vouchers along with the claims.

5. *You will clear all our payments in time along with reimbursement of all out of pocket expenses as per our standard policies and terms.*
6. *All our standard Terms and Conditions would be applicable. A copy of our standard terms is attached for your reference.*
7. *All IPR in the research reports will vest with us and the same cannot be reproduced without our approval.*
8. *Please send us a copy of your last audited accounts, your tax number, your company registration and a copy of your Memorandum and Articles for client due diligence, which is needed as per Inland Revenue Regulations. You may be required to submit such additional documents from time to time as may be required by State or Federal Agencies.*
9. *Please specify the contact person and his/her details with whom our team will coordinate. From our side I will be your contact point in R&D.*
10. *Please note that US laws will be applicable and the Courts in New York alone will have jurisdiction.*
11. *Please note that Force Majeure clause will only be applicable in our case and will not be applicable to you as you are an interested party and Acts of God are Acts in which you have a vested interest and hence there could be conflict of interest.*

Best Regards,
Ronald Mclaren

CC: Donald Duven

Ronald reads the mail carefully again and again, corrects sentences and spellings and finally decides to send it. He seeks a receipt confirmation.

'Hmmm, what's his email ID. Yes, Peter@pearlygates.hvn,' he mumbles to himself and clicks on send.

Ronald is happy as he sees the confirmation report that the mail has been sent and receipt acknowledged instantaneously. He now hopes that there will be a positive response. Whatever is the game plan of Peter and whoever the end client is, a forty million dollars plus deal would be one of their larger deals with potential of becoming the largest, once they go into implementation mode. He calculates his bonus and is pretty pleased with the number. Maybe he can plan to lease that small jet plane he has been longing for. Donald has one and if he too can have his own jet his wife would stop complaining. Something to die for!! Would he opt for Heaven if he dies? The thought crosses his mind. He is unsure. Maybe he should study the research report before making up his mind.

Donald reads the mail sent by Ronald to Peter, which is marked to him too. He calls Ronald.

'Ronald, I would like to see if this guy really transfers the first instalment of ten million. Then we shall talk. Incidentally we have received a notice from the Inland Revenue asking for Tax Registration number of this guy who has transferred the million dollars. I have sent the notice to our tax lawyers. They asked me a few questions and I sounded quite foolish not being able to answer any of them convincingly. Inland Revenue suspects the million dollar transfer may be a case of money laundering and have cautioned us to be careful. They can't trace any bank in the US called LAXMI. It could be some small, unknown bank in some tax haven. When you write again to this St Peter—I wonder what his real name is—ask him for his Tax Registration number. I tried searching Heaven Inc and St Peter on Google and there were millions of sites. Not one of them was able to throw any light on their economic strength. Their strength I believe is in prayers. Oh God, how do you deal with this phenomenon.'

'Yes Donald, I have already asked him for tax details in my mail.'

The next day Ronald jumps with joy as he reads a mail from St Peter stating that he confirms the mandate to study all systems and operations in Heaven and Hell and to do a market survey on earth to understand the mindset of people. He confirms that research approach on what people are looking forward to in the afterlife, what would motivate them to opt for Heaven and what they would be willing to sacrifice to enter the portals of Heaven is correctly understood. His covering note is brief and so is the pointwise response which reads:

R,

Thank you for your mail which did indicate that a lot of effort has gone into understanding the issues and it generally meets our requirement. With regard to your other issues, my response is as follows:

1. *Confirming the mandate.*
2. *Yes. USD 10 million being transferred into your account.*
3. *Please send the draft/signing copies.*

4. Yes.

5. No Problem.

6. Yes.

7. No problem.

8. Hmm. We live in a Tax Heaven, so there is no Tax number. Audited Accounts, MoA, Company Registration. Let me see. It's not really the way we function. So can we avoid this please.

9. I will be your contact person.

10. The Judgement of all on earth is finally on the Judgement day. Do you really want New York Courts to decide on issues concerning higher courts? Courts that will decide their fate?

11. We do not force anything major or minor. It's all decided by the laws of Nature and there are no Acts of God. Be that as it may we have no issues on you having it your way.

I may add that I have not read any of your lengthy attachments on SOPs or Terms. I assume these would be fair.

Regards
Peter

Ronald excitedly tells Donald that he has received a confirmation email and the bank has called to tell him that a large amount of $10 million has been received in the corporate account and they are proposing that the funds be parked in their new Private Equity Fund. They would like to send their Senior VP to discuss the deployment of the funds.

Donald does not seem one bit excited. He instead is nervous and sounds very worried. He has never seen such a large transfer of funds as an advance from an unknown party. He had believed that the client was some kind of a weirdo who probably had inherited a large estate and was just out to have some fun, or was probably representing some competing consultancy firm to ridicule their company. He had played along because of the enthusiasm of Ronald who had religiously believed that St Peter did indeed represent some unknown, unlisted company called Heaven Inc.

'True, this guy Peter, or St Peter if you please, is loaded with green bucks and is probably some kind of a hoax or just a kinky loaded gambler, but what he is asking for is plain stupid. We know the real St Peter. We have grown up hearing stories of God, Heaven and St Peter. We respect and revere him. But this guy is not St Peter. If he indeed was, he would not need any help from us. Heaven in fact should have all the answers, unless Heaven wants to test us, which I don't believe makes sense. In any case I don't believe in all this Heaven and Hell crap. You know that I am a non-believer. Let's assume for a moment that this is for real. How on earth are we going to conduct a survey in Heaven, or in Hell? Research on earth, yes. We could put together some template, sub-contract to marketing agencies and then come up with some analytical report using various non-linear models and statistical theorems and Google analytics to make realistic projections,' states Donald matter of factly, 'but Heaven, no way.'

Ronald responds, 'As long as St Peter keeps transferring the money, a way can be found to reach out to Heaven or Hell. Finding volunteers is only a matter of quoting the right price. Haven't you heard of jihadis willing to die for some virgins in heaven? A forty-million dollar consultancy for a one-year job! That is almost twice the size of our last consultancy contract for GE! And a million dollars paid just to prepare a mandate document!! Wow, I wish there were more such fools in this world calling themselves St Peter!!! Hope our next client is God himself paying us a billion dollars to advise Him on how to manage His kingdom.'

Ronald also indicates that they should get cracking with the full form agreement where he would build in bonuses for timely delivery. They could notch up a further twenty million dollars through bonuses. He would form teams through their worldwide network and cover geographical dispersal including US, UK, Spain, Germany, India, Japan, Russia, China, Israel, Indonesia, Saudi Arabia. This would cover the section of Catholics, Protestants, Muslims, Hindus, Jews, Buddhists and the non-believers as required by St Peter. He would ensure appropriate segmentation and send out the questionnaire and templates over the week. He says he has asked St Peter for a follow-up meeting on Wednesday.

One week later, Peter is back on the 113th floor of the Vampire Estate Building. This time there are instructions at security not to frisk Peter and to escort him.

Vanessa receives St Peter with a broad smile and escorts him into the conference room.

'Sir, Ronald will be here in a minute. Can I get you something to drink.'

'Sure, orange juice would be fine.'

'Sir, are you really St Peter—the one who would meet us at the Pearly gates?'

'Why do you doubt that? Someday I shall hopefully see you, my child, in my office, not yours.'

'No, I don't want to die. Not soon. I am happy on earth.'

'Sure, but Heaven is even better.'

'Have you seen God?'

'You don't see God. You only sense Him. Don't you sense God? Seeing is only one of the senses. Sensing engages all your senses, not just the five you recognize.'

'Yes, of course, sir. Let me get you your juice.'

Ronald walks in with two other senior executives and his laptop.

'Good morning, Sir. Hope Vanessa is taking good care of you. Let me introduce Barry and John. They will be working closely with me on this project. This is Peter, Saint Peter, who represents our client.'

They exchange greetings.

'Let me just connect this laptop and I shall take you through the presentation.'

As they all settle down, Vanessa too joins them.

Ronald takes St Peter through a presentation that include various slides:

- The Client
- The Mandate
- The Macro Objectives to be Achieved
- The Micro Objectives to be Achieved
- The Research Methodology
- The Universe Targeted
- The Sample Size

- The Sample Dispersal and Segmentation
- The Questionnaire
- The Supporting Research
- The Resource Deployment
- The Study at the Client End
- The Inputs needed from the Client
- The Timelines
- The First Draft
- The Discussions on the First Draft
- The Course Correction post Client Inputs
- The Detailed Study Phase
- The Data Compilation and Analysis
- The Statistical Models and their Explanation
- Meaningful Reporting
- The Action Points
- The Suggested Measures
- Presentation of the Report
- Feedback
- The Execution of Accepted Proposals
- Implementation Issues
- The Cost Structures
- The Warranties and Guarantees
- The Concerns
- The Confidentiality issues
- The Final Report
- The Summary Report
- Conclusions and Recommendations

As Ronald takes St Peter through the presentation he explains the details of each issue. St Peter listens carefully, interjects on a few occasions with comments and suggestions, but generally accepts the proposed line of action.

Ronald is particularly keen on seeing the reaction of Peter on the cost issue.

St Peter seems least concerned about the costs. He wants to focus on the work and its implementation. When Ronald persists on the costing to gauge the seriousness of the client and his capacity to pay, Peter responds by saying, 'Oh that's not much of a bother. I want to gift you with a lot more invaluables, but you obviously choose to put a tag on what you would like. The tag is just a number. A number that I pass to the bank, and they fill your account. It makes you happy. Actually it won't keep you happy for long. Money brings with it its own problems. And you can't cart it around with you in your afterlife. I was offering you values that would go with you wherever whenever. But have it your way. I can live with it if you can.'

'So I take it that the costs are acceptable and the first instalment will be paid soon to activate the consultancy?'

'Done,' says Peter.

A week later Ronald sends a voluminous 400-page agreement prepared by their lawyers to be signed by Heaven Inc. indemnifying R&D against any claims or litigation and on copyright matters claiming all copyright to their research and suggestions. There are also confidentiality clauses and directors' indemnity. There are long clauses on litigations, jurisdictions, arbitrations, etc.

St Peter finds the documents very unnerving. He has dealt with no such documents in the past and indicates his discomfort signing off such documents. Ronald advises him to appoint a corporate lawyer. St Peter states that there are no lawyers in Heaven. Ronald states that he could recommend a good firm of lawyers.

In the meeting with the lawyers recommended by Ronald, St Peter is asked to first sign a non-disclosure agreement. The lawyers indicate what they would do to protect the interest of their clients, but produce further lengthy documentation that would bind Heaven, its associates, subsidiaries, directors, employees, heirs, agents and representatives to follow instructions given by the legal firm from time to time to Heaven Inc. and its lawfully empowered representatives.

The forms require St Peter to indicate the name of the Chairman of Heaven Inc.

Saint Peter fills in 'GOD'.

Against the name of the Father of God, St Peter mentions 'Not known'. On the insistence that this is a compulsory field, Peter fills in 'God Father'.

St Peter wants to know whether the binding conditions will also apply to God. The lawyers recognize God only as the Chairman of Heaven Inc. and state that all dos and don'ts will apply to an executive chairman just as any functionary in charge of the company. Only in the case of non-executive chairmen would there be some exemptions. St Peter is perturbed and decides against using the legal firm and decides to sign off the consultancy agreement without the advice or approval of the legal firm.

Two weeks later Ronald and Donald along with their Sr VP (legal) are seen in the conference room of R&D Consultants at their global HQ in New York on the 113th floor of the Vampire Estate Building. As St Peter and St Paul are escorted and ushered in by Vanessa, they all stand up.

Ronald welcomes Peter and introduces his chairman. Peter introduces his colleague Paul and both take seats on opposite sides of the table.

Ronald welcomes them, makes the standard introductions and takes them through a presentation explaining the modalities of how the research would be conducted. He explains the various templates and the questions formulated to elicit meaningful responses from a cross section of the population. The segmentation would cover a sample of people from diverse religions, socio-economic status, educational backgrounds and geographical dispersal. The questionnaires would elicit responses on people's aspirations and ambitions in life, their material and spiritual desires, the afterlife expectations, the preparedness for afterlife, the compulsions while choosing between good and evil, the extent to which compromises could be made to achieve their ambitions, how they perceive Hell and Heaven, and which would be their preferred choice and why.

Ronald indicates that they are not aware where Heaven and Hell are located, do not find them in the maps but would need their team to visit Heaven and Hell to understand the structuring, operations, systems, communications and staffing so that they are able to make meaningful suggestions on restructuring and improving efficiencies and effectiveness of the same.

St Peter replies that he cannot ensure a visit to Hell. The gates of Hell are not controlled by him. He could assist with Heaven provided the team qualifies to enter the gates of Heaven. Ronald asks whether the team would need a visa and enquires about travelling arrangements. St Peter replies that the team just needs to die. They will take care of the rest.

Sr VP (legal) intervenes to say that that is not part of the contract. Vanessa is taking notes on her laptop and giggles. She hopes the Sr VP (legal) is part of the team. Her smile broadens as St Peter states that the team cannot be sent back. No one returns. It will be a one-way ticket. Either they are allowed entry to Heaven or they can go to Hell. They can however send their report down to earth. There is stunned silence all around. Donald does not understand whether St Peter is joking or serious.

Ronald says they may not be able to find any volunteers. St Peter states that he would expect R&D's team to carry out a study of Heaven to prepare a meaningful report. Sr VP (legal) points out that there is no clause for the research team to be sent outside the jurisdiction of earth and a force majeure clause and acts of God are not covered under the agreement. Death would be seen as an act of God.

St Peter states that he does not understand any legal jargon. The agreement was not shown to any lawyer as there are no lawyers in Heaven. He has signed in good faith and hopes R&D will deliver on the promise. Ronald offers to do the study of Heaven on earth itself. He states they would put a heavenly team in place, but they would need capable persons from Heaven to respond to their queries and hold one-on-one interviews. St Peter states that he, St Paul and his team would be able to answer all questions relating to Heaven.

A date for the meeting is set up.

❄❄❄

The Functioning of Heaven

R&D executives spend a considerable amount of time trying to understand how Heaven functions, the Systems and Standard Operating Processes in place, roles and responsibilities, delegation of power, how departments are structured, control and regulatory mechanisms, conflict resolution modalities, procedure for selecting those who are shortlisted to die, the entry bars and barriers to Heaven, the rights and obligations, perks and privileges in Heaven.

The consultants send a long list of questions to be answered and forms to be filled up by various departments in Heaven. They insist that every god heading a functional department fill up a detailed form giving insight into the functioning of the department to give R&D the needed understanding to analyze the operations.

St Peter and St Paul are interviewed at length over days consisting of many sittings to understand the functioning of Heaven.

St Peter explains the process at length: 'The soul is born soon after the fertilization of the egg in the womb. The soul is in the form of plasma, spread along the contours of the body and grows with the body. Over the years the soul assimilates the characteristics of the individual, however it is at all times distinct from the body. It has no escape from the body until the heart stops beating. Once the heart stops and the body ceases to function, the soul is liberated from the body and assumes its own independent existence. The soul is weightless and has no density but retains the contours and functions of the body. It has a consciousness of its own and has a life as if the body had transposed itself and its characteristics into the soul. It is however far superior to the body and when liberated from the body it has an infinite existence. It is immortal, indestructible and timeless. It cannot decay or age, cannot be affected by disease or attack and can travel in space and time at will, achieving speeds upto the speed of light. It can carry on all bodily functions and can be as young or as old as it desires. The soul reflects the values and spirit of the individual.

'God has not retained unto Himself the power to decide on life or death as is generally perceived. God does not decide when a person dies. In fact this power was desired by the Devil and he moved Heaven and earth to try and be the decision maker on when a person should die. This would have given him enormous power over humans. But God willed otherwise. He insisted that the laws of nature determine the time of death. The laws ensure that a person dies of old age unless the death is premature owing to accident, ill health, natural calamities or violence. Accidents are a result of people disobeying the laws of nature; calamities are a result of natural forces at play in the evolutionary process and people being caught in the midst of these forces; illness is a result of the struggle for survival of various life forms with natural selection being at work within the body; and finally violence is the Devil at work through the minds he is able to influence.

'When the soul is liberated from the body, it is escorted by the Angels (Yamdoots) to Heaven. During the journey all rights and obligations post death are explained to the soul along with the options available to it. The soul is briefed by Angels of its rights and obligations in Heaven if admitted, and the options available if not admitted. The emissaries of the Devil have an opportunity to explain the offerings in Hell if the soul is interested in it. In case the soul opts to go to Hell, it is free to do so. Souls that do not find their way to Heaven or opt for Hell become gargolytes that are forever roaming aimlessly in the cosmos.

'At the Gates of Heaven the soul is met by me or St Paul or any of our emissaries, and presented in the Hall of Judgement. There on the Day of the Judgement, the conduct and contribution of the soul while on earth is evaluated. There are no fixed guidelines or rules for entry unto Heaven. The panel of Judges only follows one touchstone: has the soul contributed meaningfully and honestly to the betterment of fellow earthlings or has the person lived for himself and harmed others.

'From kings to paupers, all are treated equally. There are no VIPs.

'There is no value assigned to the wealth of the individual or to the awards he may have been conferred on earth. It is not the tangibles that are evaluated.

'The soul is given a chance to present all its good deeds or any value addition to the life of others. The soul has access to full memory recall. Claims of the soul can be substantiated or refuted by a virtual replay of events as they happened. Often souls learn about their real contribution as opposed to their perceived contribution during such replays. What is evaluated on the Judgement Day are the invaluables that cannot be measured in monetary terms. People that may be highly revered on earth may not necessarily be admitted in Heaven. There are hardly any kings and queens, politicians and power brokers who have qualified to live in Heaven. There is not a single god man, very few religious heads, not a single jihadi or crusader, and very few earth billionaires in Heaven.

'The Judgement is based on the summation of the positive attribute quotient minus the negative attribute quotients. Positive quotients include laughter, happiness, helpfulness, politeness, selflessness, love and honesty. Negative quotients include greed, jealousy, hatred, anger, aggression, treachery. There is no appeal against the Jury's decision. If accepted the soul is welcomed as a celebrity. If consigned to the vast, empty cold space of the universe for eternity it becomes part of the cosmic plasma. If it opts to return to earth it can do so either in a lower life form after full memory wipe or enter another human body at its birth after undergoing complete memory wipe and starting *de novo*. The Indian concept of Karmic cycle is partly true and valid to the extent of the soul having the option to go back, but not in the way suggested in Vedic scriptures and not as a reward or punishment.

'Souls that are allowed to live in Heaven have to follow the Ten Commandments of Heaven. These are:

Thou shall not follow any Cult, Religion or Figurehead
Thou shall believe in and pursue only Science and Truth

Thou shall live in Peace, Love and Harmony

Thou shall not visit Earth or Hell

Thou may communicate with earthlings only through dreams and visions

Thou shall aspire to understand the origin of the cosmos and life

Thou shall have no negative emotions

Thou shall dedicate thy time so as to add value to life and environment

Thou shall respect decisions of the All Souls' Council

Thou shall respect and love all forms of life and environment

'Beyond the Ten Commandments there are no laws in Heaven, no policing, no law enforcement agencies, no defence or security forces, no governments.

'There are gods who mentor and oversee services such as prayers, entry to Heaven, conflict resolution, science and technology, research and development.

'In case of any violations, the soul is required to spend time in rehabilitation. There is no punishment in Heaven except that travel speeds can be reduced thereby restricting long space journeys by souls.

'In Heaven there is no money and no concept of monetization. Security of life and living standards are assured. Hence there is no greed and no compulsion to amass wealth or material. There is therefore no need for financial institutions or services. There is a great emphasis on value creation, on creativity, on original thinking and designing. This is not led by motivation of becoming materially richer but by the motivation of becoming intellectually and spiritually richer while contributing meaningfully in improving lives of others around. The pure satisfaction of seeing an improved environment is motivation enough.

'There is no travel and transport system in Heaven as a soul can travel at will and at speeds of light. There is therefore no pollution in Heaven. The soul can choose where it wants to live, how it wants to live, what age it wants to adopt. There is abundant space in Heaven and the soul can choose its time and space and change these at will. Heaven is the most beautiful and the largest 'planet' in the universe. It is the centre of the universe and is larger than a thousand suns.

'Souls can create a micro atmosphere around themselves and can live or sleep in nature without the concerns of weather, security or fear for life. If, however, the soul would prefer the comforts it has been used to on earth, including a home, entertainment, etc., there are atomizers and antizers. These are virtual computerized robotics that are engineering marvels that can put together atoms in the desired sequence to create homes, clothing, food or whatever the soul may desire, in an instant. These are sophisticated versions of 3D printers seen on earth. When not required, the atoms can be disintegrated by antizers, so as not to leave any waste. The only thing atomizers cannot create is life.

'To create a home, for example, a soul can feed its design into the atomizer or may even choose from among millions of available options displayed on the screen of the atomizer or create homes from combinations of various modules available.

Upon confirmation, the atomizer will put the required home where needed in a jiffy by combining the atoms and molecules in the right sequence. It's almost as if God were at work. There are no copyrights as design and knowledge are expected to be shared freely. The good of others is the motivating force, not the greed to get richer.

'Atomizers thus replace all industries and antizers keep Heaven pollution free. Souls have the option of temperature controls around their contours. This system eliminates the need for any heating or air-conditioning systems. The micro climatic contours ensure that the air layer immediately covering the contours of the soul becomes an insulating layer irrespective of the weather conditions outside. This helps the body enjoy all weathers and seasons without the need for any clothes. Nudity is accepted in Heaven and the soul has the choice of wearing or not wearing clothes. Clothes are only worn by souls initially as a sheer force of habit, but most souls over a period opt to shed them. Souls generally opt to live in a state of youth, a time when they have able bodies, although many choose middle age or old age that carry wisdom with it.

'Souls are encouraged to travel around the galaxies singly or in groups. Souls may go into hibernation during such travels since periods involved can sometimes only be measured in light years. Often all that the souls end up seeing during their space travels are barren planets. There is the gigantic cosmic library and the aid of Hoogle space for travel. Souls can choose solar systems where they may find things of their interest. They are also encouraged to do research work, probe matter, probe energies and develop technologies that can improve and better their lifestyles. Some of the technologies being used are those that were developed on earth, and although all the top minds are in Heaven the development speeds are not comparable to those on earth despite the better resource situation. It is believed that lack of competition and inadequate motivation is the main reason why even highly intelligent minds in Heaven are not pursuing research vigorously. The other reason is that a lot of thought goes into eco-sustainability so that the overall environment is not adversely affected. On earth the pace of growth is determined by greed, and concerns for the ecology are often ignored. There is little emphasis on earth on any long-term thinking.

'The fact that every soul is immortal puts no immediate pressures on any time frames.'

On being questioned why souls are not allowed to travel at speeds faster than light, nor allowed to visit the earth, Peter responds that these are not desirable.

'Travel at speeds faster than the speed of light is contrary to the laws of physics and visits to earth by souls would be unfair to those on earth. It would disturb the living and get them far too obsessed with life beyond. God wants the living to focus on their life on earth. There have been some rogue souls that have violated the law of not visiting the earth and such souls have given rise to all kinds of ghastly, or ghostly speculations.

'While souls wanting to go to earth are allowed to enter bodies provided the soul returns to earth post a memory wipe, they could land in Hell if they are not granted entry back to Heaven in their new form as they would cease to be the existing soul and the new soul avatar they adopt would end up acquiring characteristics and behavioural pattern of the new body they are in.'

It is clarified that souls in Heaven are free to pursue whatever interests they may have. These include reading, learning, entertainment, travel, experimentation, writing, recording, music, arts, medicine, engineering, environment, evolution, etc. However the most popular with souls is reliving their lives in virtual life using the what-if option. The what-if option allows one to go through life seeing how things would have been had they chosen differently at any stage of life. Souls also have the option of reading the minds of earthlings. Many souls use this power to know what their near and dear ones actually are thinking or saying about them. This can often lead to unhappiness and depression as Heaveners, much to their chagrin, realize that all is not what it seems to be.

Souls travel a lot, experiment a lot and play a lot. There is every form of sports activity available. There is dance, music, clubs, adventure sports, extreme sports; everything one can imagine. So Heaven is not such a boring place.

When questioned on sex, St Peter responds, 'Sex was created for procreation and made sufficiently rewarding for the species to pursue the same.'

'True that man has made sex into a well-developed art and sport. If man would have spent as much time in other areas of research as he does in pursuit of sex, the earth may have been a more liveable place. Man is obsessed with sex, yet he has put many artificial barriers in the game that were never intended by nature. In Heaven two or more consenting adults are free to have sex. There are no restrictions. There is no procreation in Heaven, so sex is a pure pleasure play. In the absence of procreation bondings between couples are not as strong as they are on earth. It keeps jealousies away. There is no concept of marriage and couples are free to live together as long as they are happy or move out at any time without any obligations. Bonding is not need related, as all needs are fulfilled in Heaven with little or no struggle. Bonding is more bilateral or multilateral activity related. Sex is celebrated and there is no guilt associated with sex.

'Thus the soul can continue with all its earthly activities and much more in Heaven without the stress of having to earn a living. Heaven is payback time. In the absence of money, there is no greed, people are equal, all are well off and no one is in a hurry, since everyone is immortal.

'Many of the souls express that despite all the comfort in Heaven and the problems they faced on earth, they still think very fondly of their brief period on earth and are not unwilling to risk their current life for another spell on earth. This perception is on the rise and the reasons for the same need to be understood.

'Food is not a must as souls get their energy from solar sources. However food is in abundance for souls desirous of pursuing a taste and ritual created on earth. It also provides a platform to meet and engage with each others. Souls can freely access all farm goods directly from the farm or can grow these themselves. Ownership is common. No permissions or payments are required. There are no taxes. If a soul does not feel like cooking or eating at home, there are plenty of soul-carry restaurants and fine dining restaurants of every imaginable cuisine, at no cost. Or souls can just fall back on solar energy, which is in abundance.

'All services in Heaven are run by volunteers. Souls can hear music or watch TV through the eye of the mind by focusing on the programmes they would like to watch. Programmes can be chosen from the huge central database of Multi-D HD holographic AV programmes. Souls are also free to create their own programmes and upload into the central database.

'Souls communicate long distance through mind interlocks. They just use the frequency modulator that is a built-in attribute in each soul. The communication can be audio-visual. Of course by and large souls prefer to communicate one-to-one by meeting in person. At the speed of light you can virtually be present whenever you want wherever you want anywhere in Heaven instantaneously.'

'How is Heaven structured and managed?'

'There really is not much to manage in Heaven. Souls admitted to Heaven are cultured and with good values. Since souls can travel at will and can travel upto the speeds of light there is no need for transportation systems. Since souls are matterless, there are no accidents. With no viruses, microbes or bacteria in Heaven illnesses are non existent. Age-related ailments do not exist as there is no ageing. There are therefore no hospitals or healthcare systems. Souls communicate through minds, so there are no communication systems. There is no need for money and there are no monetary systems, so no banks or financial services. So what is really there to monitor or administer?

'Yes, Heaven has schools and educational institutions in abundance, so those who want to learn, re-learn or acquire new skills and are unable to do this on their own are free to join these schools. There are huge libraries and labs of all nature and souls are encouraged to probe, question, search, research anything and everything to understand the universe and to make it a better place. Those not with scientifically inclined minds are encouraged to pursue art forms and there is a great deal of experimentation in art forms: from photography to painting, from 3D to holograms, from virtual reality to augmented reality, from dreams to visions, from music to dance, from theatre to cinema, and from opera to literature. Sports in its various forms is also encouraged and vigorously practised in Heaven. Football is the most loved sport in Heaven. Swimming, cycling, skating, skiing, athletics, base ball and cricket are the other popular sporting activities. Extreme sports are popular as there are no death risks or accidents involved.'

Ronald hears all of St Peter's explanations with awe and amazement. He still has a lingering suspicion about St Peter, the man, his antecedents and his claim of representing God, but likes the explanations St Peter is giving. He likes it even more that he has been paid in advance for a job that has just begun and may not take too much of his time or effort.

Ronald asks St Peter about Hell.

St Peter tells Ronald, 'No one has seen Hell. Any soul visiting Hell cannot come back to Heaven so very little is known of Hell though there is a lot of speculation about it. Most of the knowledge about Hell is based on Hell's marketing communications which are very unlikely to be true.

'The Devil and his team are very active on earth. They are aware that the soul takes on the attributes of the body. They therefore tempt the body through physical pleasures to which the body is very susceptible. Hell's campaign is built on "Say Yes to S cube".

'The three Ss—Sex, Substance and Stimulants—in any and all forms with no limitations, is the focus of their strategy. Sex, Substance and Stimulants were all created by God for a purpose. They all have their reason to be, but are detrimental to the body in excess or in unregulated form. Substance abuse includes drugs, alcoholism and other chemicals inducing euphoric feelings momentarily. Stimulants include abuse of money, power and violence. It is these excesses and abuses that the Devil promotes to the body and reaps in the soul.

'The youth on earth is most vulnerable to the physical pleasures, and hence forms the softer target. They are exposed to S cube, then addicted, and finally entrapped. When the soul leaves the body it leaves with the body's attributes and its addiction to S cube. Sometimes a soul may be saved when in later years there is realization by the body of the Devil's plans. Most times however it is a downhill street, a street to Hell. What is unfortunate, however, is that the marketing strategies of Hell tend to attribute virtue to this lifestyle and tends to indicate that this lifestyle can continue in Hell. So, live it up and go to Hell…by choice. Increasingly therefore more people are opting for Hell.

'No one really knows how Hell functions or what the souls do out there. We are hoping your report will throw more light on Hell and guide us on how we can combat their marketing campaigns.'

Ronald tells St Peter that he has to rush for the funeral mass of one of his clients and asks whether the rest of the discussions can be continued the next day. St Peter appreciates the concern that Ronald has for his client, but Ronald responds saying that his concern really is that William Hart Jr., the deceased, has not cleared many of his bills and he needs to be seen at the funeral to connect with the heirs as he will need to raise the claims with them sooner rather than later.

St Peter says that he knows William Hart Jr. as his soul was at the gates of Heaven a few days earlier after William died. St Peter asks Ronald if he can accompany him to the funeral mass and Ronald replies that he sees no problem provided St Peter is dressed appropriately for the occasion. St Peter tells Ronald that he will meet him outside the church in an hour, appropriately dressed.

St Peter is seen formally dressed for a crowded funeral mass as he waits for Ronald who arrives in a black Mercedes. As the two of them walk into the church, Ronald spots the widow and walks past her so as to be seen by her. He then bows before the casket, lays a wreath on it, walks up to the widow, introduces himself and offers his condolences while eulogizing William.

St Peter follows Ronald.

Elizabeth the widow looks at St Peter and knows that he is different. She feels that there is something divine about St Peter but is unsure. She acknowledges his condolences. The formal rites begin and the bishop takes the pulpit.

'Today we say goodbye to the only child of Joseph and Jennifer. Bill will be remembered for a long long time not only as a big dreamer and achiever but also as one who has helped many others achieve their dreams. He lived a life by principles and died for them. His life was not an easy one, but he himself was made of sterner stuff and obstacles of life did little to slow him down. He found ways and means to overcome these or to pass by them, but never did he let them dampen his spirits or his will to achieve the goals he set for himself.

'He was a caring husband and a loving father to his two teenaged children, Paul and Martha. He made sure that they were all well provided for and has left behind an estate that would serve them well. He started life as a humble trader, but through the dint of his hard work and the blessings of the Almighty he reached the dizzying heights of the corporate world. As CEO of one of the valued American companies he was highly respected and was much sought after for advice and guidance. His friends, many of whom are here today, loved him and admired him and to them the family can look towards in their difficult times. Whatever he did he did for others and with the welfare of the people at large at heart. His two published books have been greatly admired by critics and readers alike and are today used as textbooks in management schools. He shall be remembered by students of management as a person who gave them the magical five Theta formula of success.

'We know that Bill, who was a committed father and a loyal husband to Elizabeth, must now be on the way to the gates of Heaven. We are sure that God Almighty would receive him with open arms for all the good that he has done on earth and we pray to Jesus that Bill, William Hart Jr., be blessed for his generosity and love for fellow human beings and be given shelter under the benign umbrella of the Lord. May his soul rest in peace. Amen.'

As the family walks past the casket to the pulpit to offer their obituaries, St Peter whispers to Ronald, 'It's a pity he did not make it to Heaven. Such a difference between the earthly perception and the truth!'

Ronald seems perplexed.

'For all that has been said here and probably believed, Bill was neither loyal nor faithful to his wife. In fact at least two of the women he was having an affair with are here in this church. As regards his success, he was really ruthless. He used every trick in the trade and broke every rule to have his way. His daughter in fact wanted to commit suicide. She hated her father for treating her the way he did when she was in love with her boyfriend Tom. The money he made and the estate he built was all by manipulation of shares including what you call insider trading. Half of his so-called friends are actually his bitter rivals or enemies who just had to put up with him and pretended to like him because of his position of power. The books that he wrote were ghost written by paid writers.'

Ronald is shocked and can't believe most of what St Peter is saying though he himself has envied the rise of William and was in fact jealous of his success. His bigger concern is that William had not kept his promise of awarding Ronald the consultancy contract that he had pitched for and had instead given it to their rivals. Ronald was aware that William had asked for a cut for the consultancy job and could not have been a principled man. A part of the cut had been paid to William in anticipation of the contract. The balance was to be paid upon the award of the contract. William had defaulted and given the contract to their rivals. Though William had promised to return the advance of the cut and promised to give them another contract, he had done neither. Now here was his dead body and everyone was talking highly of him. William had received several peer and industry awards hailing him to be an outstanding entrepreneur and businessman and a high achiever. They could not all be wrong.

'Yes, they could all be wrong,' said St Peter, as if reading Ronald's mind.

'In Heaven none of these things are considered. You do not go there with any earthly certificate of merit or achievement. You go there naked just the way you came. Your soul just carries your deeds with you. The truth is crystal clear and it is there for all to see. There is no window dressing. Based on the facts, Bill was rejected a place in Heaven.

'It's a pity that he is presently rotting in Hell while his eulogies are being read on earth and the Lord being praised in the hope that he will be received with open arms in Heaven. Even I am impressed by all that has been said here today and would have been easily taken in by the bishop's statements had I not known the truth. It's a pity that I had met Bill's soul just a few days ago in Heaven. And now here I am, a part of his funeral mass, hearing lies and nothing but untruths. I wonder how much of all this the bishop himself believes. The irony is that the bishop himself has a lot to hide. Here everyone is revering him, while he behind closed doors is indulging in unmentionables. But that is another story.'

***

R&D's Report

After extensive discussions with St Peter, St Paul, Angel Gabriel and others Ronald sits down with his team to discuss the structure of the report. There is confusion and uncertainty about a whole lot of issues. As religious books including the Koran, Bible, Geeta and others are analyzed they seem to be incongruent with scientific thought and knowledge. There are vast inconsistencies, contradictions and unsubstantiated statements bordering on superstition and the ridiculous. Yes, any contradiction based on established facts or theories run the danger of being blasphemous. It is clear that not only is Hell running a major campaign to influence young minds but Heaven too is running a campaign through its ambassadors full of falsehood and untruths being passed off as the gospel truth. The facts about Heaven as spelt out during discussions with St Peter and his team are very different from those being propagated on earth. Yes, a massive course correction is needed in the brand recognition, brand positioning, attributes and desirability of Heaven as an attractive option of post-life living. Yet, it's going to be a big challenge letting Heaven know that it is being run all wrong and is being marketed even worse.

After a lot of discussions, arguments and altercations, R&D executives conclude that they need more primary data and need to prepare an improved template to collate further empirical perception data and responses of people across the globe in different socio-economic strata, age groups and religious beliefs.

Among the questions that require the respondents to apply their minds include:

- Do they practise Religion? If so which is the faith they follow?
- Do they believe in God?
- Which God do they believe in?
- At what age do they expect to die?
- Do they believe in Heaven and Hell?
- What is their perception of life in Heaven?
- What is their perception of life in Hell?
- Where would they choose to spend their afterlife and why?
- If they had an option would they rather live on earth?
- What perks and privileges would attract them to Heaven?
- Under what circumstances would they prefer Hell over Heaven?
- Under what circumstances would they prefer Heaven over Hell?

To ensure they get a response, a gift hamper is offered to each one filling up the questionnaire.

Interviews are conducted online, via social media, through mobile surveys extensively and across geographical areas ensuring detailed discussions with people claiming near-death experiences. Interviews are often recorded where the client has no objection to a record being kept and is willing to agree to release terms, thus protecting R&D against any possible future litigation relating to privacy infringement.

Meetings with those who claim to have seen ghosts are held and their experiences recorded wherever permitted. Those claiming to remember their past lives are questioned at length to gather as much information as possible on their memory between the two lives. Religious leaders and scholars are interviewed. Communities believing in the Devil and running hell societies are questioned. Godmen are interviewed at length. Every single word on Heaven and Hell thrown up by Google is studied. Exorcist societies are studied and their promoters interviewed. Graveyard societies are roped in to assist with their views. Cults aligned with Hell or the Devil are extensively tapped for information.

The information collected runs into hundreds of thousands of pages. The entire available data and response is fed into the computer and analyzed through various models using sophisticated statistical software, keywords and analytics. The data is analyzed by teams to chalk out a discernable pattern.

A whole research team led by renowned statisticians works round the clock to examine various hypothesis, studying sensitivity analysis and coming out with meaningful findings that fit with projected hypothesis and promise relatively low error margins.

From out of reams and reams of data, charts, graphs, excel sheets and apparently logical assumptions evolve a voluminous report on the functioning of Heaven and Hell. The SWOT analysis, the pull and push factors, the market positioning, the desire and demand, the way forward and the strategies suggested to deal with the problem are given shape.

Finally Ronald walks into Donald's room a few months before the fast approaching deadline of submission of the report.

'Donald, I have with me the first draft of the SWOT analysis on Heaven. I have completed the analysis based on details provided by St Peter and others, the response to the questionnaire, and our own research. We have come up with suggestions and recommendations, and I would like you to have a look at the same to know your views. Once I have them I will work on the final report to be sent to the client.

'Our problem however is that we have no authentic data or information on Hell. While we had St Peter, Paul and his team to give us first-hand information on the functioning of Heaven, and enough supporting data from the questionnaire sent out, we have been unable to find a single soul that has been to Hell and back. There have been many fakes who claimed to have visited Hell but we can't go by their versions. There has been no way to get in touch with the Devil or his cronies. Whatever information we have is based on our Google search, perceptions of people, and description of Hell as provided in the Holy Scriptures. We have a fairly voluminous feedback from a diverse sample of target groups on their perception of Hell, their attraction or repulsion on a scale of zero to ten, and association of emotions with words that have a strong linkage with Hell. However, none of this has primary authentication and would not stand scrutiny by standards of International Research Reporting. We even connected with fans of Hell groups and members of devil nights, evil societies, Lucifer clubs, graveyard groups, as also those indulging in devilish rituals, but all of the feedback is based on the individual's own belief system or cult beliefs. Of course, the respondents are completely concerned about life in the nether world and believe all of what they say to be the absolute truth. What do you suggest we do?'

'Look Ronald, we don't have much time. We are working against deadlines. The final report has to reach our clients by the end of the year. That leaves us with just about four months. I suggest you base your analysis of Hell on the feedback you already have. Do a good deal of window dressing with mathematical projections so it's not difficult for the client to lap up the information as authentic. We have done it in the past and clients have not been any the wiser. They will accept anything thrown at them as long as it is what they want to believe. What they are really seeking is a reputed brand like ours endorsing the data and analysis. That's what we are providing. That's what we are paid for. When R&D says something in a report the world sits up and pays attention. Markets move up or down based on our reports. Moneybags invest moolah based on our reports. So just make the report look authentic and f**k the content. It's the packaging, not the product that is important. And yes, in the source credits, do mention all those crazy guys who claim those near-death experiences or those who insist that they have been to Hell and back as reliable sources. Keep on record a psychiatrist's report certifying them to be sane and rational individuals who have not been delusional or hallucinating while talking of their experiences. We don't have much time left. So just wind it up now. Your report in any case will run into thousands of pages. Who the hell is going to read it all, up there in Heaven? To me the whole thing sounds like one big joke. I can't believe we are actually doing this. I would never have taken up this assignment but for the guy's paying the money upfront. This may all just be one big hoax. But I don't care. We have our money and that's what matters. We are still facing issues with the Inland Revenue on the source of the fund transfer and I am having to pay heavy amounts to our tax consultants to keep the Inland Revenue guys at bay.

'The clients, whoever they are, will probably just read your section on conclusions and recommendations. Yes, that's the part of the report I want to go through. The rest is ruffage. Just ensure that you lavish praise on St Peter and his cronies in your acknowledgements. Reports are loved by those who are credited prominently therein! They almost take over the ownership of the report and that helps. Praise anyone else you need to. Praise the Lord. The chapter on acknowledgements is always read. If anyone is missed out, your report will be under fire from that person. So give credit even where it is not due. I hope you have been looking after Peter and his team well. Which hotel are they staying in? Take good care of him. You know what I mean. Ask that escort service to send the best of their escorts to take care of Peter and his team and fulfil all their wishes and desires. And I mean, all.'

Ronald leaves some documents with Donald and tells him that these are some of his early conclusions. It would help if Donald went through them and gave him a response.

Donald studies the conclusions. The conclusions include:

a) While the belief in the existence of Heaven among earthlings is strong there is insufficient understanding of what Heaven offers apart from it being a place where gods live and it being an abode where do-gooders can coexist with the gods.

b) No one seems to be clear whether they would be accepted in Heaven and what they can expect if they are accepted in Heaven.

c) There seems to be a general perception that there are no communication lines between Heaven and earth as no one seems to have been able to speak to those in Heaven. If they do exist, the communication lines are one way with prayers reaching Heaven without there being any response.

d) Hell has done a much better job of marketing and convincing people that Hell is a fun place. The brand association of Hell with youth, fun and unrestricted action is strong. Hell as a place full of fires is increasingly being perceived as a fear being introduced by religious bodies and leaders to create anxiety and buy loyalty for Heaven. The fear factor is wearing off among the more educated and Hell is an option that is no longer being discarded outright. Anything hot is good. Girls that are hot are good. Fire is hot, so fire is good!

e) Devil is far more accessible and acceptable particularly to the younger people. They tend to believe that they can aspire to become little Devils themselves or be his cronies but cannot aspire to become God or the Angels. The aspirations of Hell seem more achievable.

f) The perception among people is that Hell has fewer dos, don'ts and restrictions. People do not like restrictions. They do not like to be told what they can or cannot do. They do not like places where there are restrictions.

g) There is a general belief that one can run with the Devil all through life and finally say one last prayer or perform some ritual, a holy river bath, pilgrimage or penance in old age to wipe off all the sins and embrace Heaven as a choice for the final abode. The belief that God is far more forgiving is strong. The last minute penance route to Heaven has taken away the need to have any long term loyalty to Heaven.

h) There is total confusion among earthlings on the hierarchy and multiplicity of gods. No one is clear who they need to go to for any specific need and often they are barking (read praying) up the wrong tree. There is no clarity on whether there is one God or many. There is no clarity on whether gods of different religions are indeed the same by different names or they are indeed different and probably at war with each other as their followers on earth are. There is a widespread belief of one's god being superior to the other's.

i) The hierarchy in Hell is clearer with the Devil being the sole and supreme commander. Earthlings believe it would be easier to deal with Hell given the clear hierarchy of command. People like clarity. People like a distinctly identifiable leader.

j) The self-appointed brokers of God on earth have created a large number of religions and aggrandized power unto themselves projecting that they truly represent the gods and the way to Heaven is through them. Some of these agents even call themselves godmen. Heaven has taken no steps to dispel this belief or to nullify the misguidance of the so called godmen who earthlings believe are middlemen distancing them from God rather than bringing them closer to Him.

k) Killings in the name of God are generally deemed to be acceptable and are counted as bonus points by many to reach Heaven. The concept of the one believing in a god which is different from the one you believe in, being a heathen or a *kafir* or a devil is widespread. The sanction to kill the kafir comes from the religious leaders who gain by diverting anger against others while they bask in glory in the name of their gods.

l) There is a perception that very beautiful women (apsaras) welcome you in Heaven but you cannot touch them, while in Hell you can be interactive with the bad girls. Men prefer active bad girls in Hell to pious women in Heaven and find this a strong motivation to opt for Hell. Surprisingly women prefer to be where they perceive their men are likely to be. There is a perception that sex is not permissible in Heaven and that there is free sex including orgies permitted in Hell. This is a major motivation for young male adults to opt for Hell. Women are not found to be averse to the choice of Hell and are not disturbed by sex or orgies in

Hell. The perception of virgins by the dozens waiting in Heaven for those who have committed jihad in the name of god leads to questions about the source of so many virgins. Apparently, after their virginity is lost their role seems to cease and therefore they probably are sent to Hell. Other younger non-jihadi males seem happy to settle for the non-virgins in Hell.

m) Given a choice most people would prefer youth on earth as the first choice. Youth in Hell is their second choice. Old age on earth is their third choice and old age in Heaven is the last choice. The problem is that even in their eighties people tend to believe that they are young enough to be in Hell. Among those in their nineties very few demonstrated the understanding of the questions or the problems well enough and their responses could not be given much weightage.

n) There seems to be very little clarity on immortality and what it means. How would time be spent if one is immortal? What activities can keep you engaged for years, hundreds of years, thousands of years, for eternity? Would the excitement last or would boredom and fatigue step in? Isn't death as a final solution a better option with no gods or Heaven or Hell to deal with?

After studying the findings and other reports left behind by Ronald, Donald makes his notes and later sends out his recommendations.

The recommendations suggested by Donald include:

a) Heaven needs to be marketed as a fun place, not as a pious one.
b) Fun or pleasure should not be deemed to be evil as long as it does not hurt others.
c) Heaven be rebranded as an adventure zone where youth, good health, high energy levels are ensured and there are no monetary worries.
d) Option of sexual outlet in the absence of spouse/ companion who may still be on earth should be available and the same be marketed appropriately. The availability of sex was among male respondents the single most desirable reason to choose the life-after abode. The sex policy in Heaven must be clarified. Sex with a non spouse or a new companion should be permissible and not be deemed to be a sin or a debarred activity. (It does seem from the responses of St Peter that this is the case but the perception among the TG is different.)
e) 1-800-PRAYER needs to be introduced with a pro-active call centre to give better comfort levels to clients.
f) Restoration of youth and beauty upon reaching Heaven is the single most desirable attribute to opt for Heaven among female respondents. This must be assured. Females want to look young, beautiful and be sexually attractive.
g) The confusion of rebirth in lower forms needs to be dispelled and the emphasis should be on youth and

immortality with pleasurable options better than those available on earth.

h) Heaven should consider appointing a CEO, so that there is better coordination between the various departments and gods.

i) A marketing strategy that revolves around a new logo, a new catchline, 'SAY YES TO HEAVEN', be launched.

A jingle, music video and marketing campaign around the verse below may be created indicating the kind of 360 degree marketing campaign that needs to be launched.

Hell, it's time you sought a better life
No worries, no hassles, no stress, no strife
For fun and joy with love and happiness
Not New York or Paris, nor London or Venice
It's where flows freely, good food and wine
Where Music and Dance and Sex is all fine
Pretty hostesses to serve, just ask for your choice
You can romance, dance or drink for no price
Think of the best and multiply it by seven
That's what you can expect when you come to Heaven
SAY YES to HEAVEN

***

Discussions on the Report

About an earth year after the assembly in the Hall of Thoughts where the issue of rapidly declining market share in souls was discussed, the gods have now reassembled to assess the report submitted by R&D Consultants.

God himself is not present.

The atmosphere is relaxed and informal.

St Peter calls the meeting to order, apologizes that God is not there but reiterates that he is present even in his absence. He also indicates that God has urged the assembly to discuss the report threadbare and take appropriate decisions. St Peter then proceeds to present the report submitted by R&D. St Peter rewinds to the dilemma being faced by Heaven, the concerns of souls preferring Hell and the wrong perception of Heaven in the minds of earthlings. He speaks about the decision to appoint a leading consultancy on earth to examine all relevant issues and recommend changes and action points to Heaven. He reads out the relevant parts of the R&D Consultants' observations, analysis and recommendations.

After hearing the detailed presentation by St Peter on R&D's report there is a silence in the auditorium. It is unclear whether the gods are impressed with the report or are upset.

St Peter is holding his breath. He is expecting an applause. There is none.

After a pregnant pause, during which there is some discernible unease all around, a few responses come forward. The responses are guarded in relation to recommendations concerning the responder's own department but there is perceptible acceptance in relation to the suggestions concerning other departments. There is shock expressed on some of the recommendations relating to free sexual activity being used as a marketing tool.

The thought of appointment of a CEO in Heaven meets general disapproval.

There is general concern expressed about the fact that Hell is using unfair trade practices to enhance its market share.

There is a suggestion that senses and the sensory nerves in human beings be redesigned so that it does not fall prey to the S cube.

St Peter reminds those assembled that God of course believes that the Human should be able to rise above the temptations to make informed choices on what is good and relevant for him. If the Devil is misusing man's weakness by misleading him through misguided marketing strategies, the response should not be to change the structural design that is not at fault, but to counter the marketing strategy.

'You should therefore suggest strategies to counter those of the Devil, though any suggestions on change in the structural design of the Human body or mind may also be considered,' adds St Peter.

The report of R&D indicates that the sample size is fairly large and representative. It is agreed that there is need to discuss the report with the All Souls' Council that represents the souls that have experienced both Heaven and earth. It is suggested that members of the Council be requested to join the debate.

St Peter sends a thought message and almost instantly many of the members of the All Souls' Council start gliding into the auditorium.

We see about a 100 souls coming in and among these are Albert Einstein, Nelson Mandela, Mother Teresa and Gandhi. The President of the All Souls' Council is Gandhi. He rises to thank St Peter for the opportunity to meet them after a very long period of time and expresses that it would be desirable for God to meet the Council as well. He states that souls have come to Heaven hoping to see God and interact with Him more often. Of course they do meet His emissaries often, but His own interaction would make a difference.

St Peter states that with Gandhi himself being there why does anyone need to meet God. He has shown the world how to live and let live and his example has been by far the best, better than what many of His emissaries who were sent to earth were able to accomplish. In fact if Gandhi was inclined, God would like to send him back as His emissary to earth. Gandhi declines and states that what he had to tell the world he already has. There is nothing new he has to offer. The world needs time to realize its own follies and the wrong path it is following.

It is generally agreed that lack of good political, social and religious leadership is what is missing but this leadership must emerge from the people themselves and not be imposed by

Heaven. The current earth leadership is high on decibels and low on depth of thinking.

As souls that have lived in bodies on earth he urges them to give their feedback on whether the aspirations of souls in Heaven have been fulfilled and if and what changes they would like to see.

Gandhi states that he himself is very satisfied with Heaven. There is peace, love and equality. There is unending scope for reading, development of the mind, introspection and research. However he is aware that there is a fair amount of discontentment among many souls and he would encourage them to speak up. He goads several souls to speak up and also adds to their views from time to time as many souls stand up to speak their minds.

The gist of their grievances is that souls do not have much to do as Heaven is a very comfortable place and there are no pressures, no survival compulsions. The souls are expected to create their own activities. The predictability also adds to their boredom.

There is a fair amount of logically argued discussion on the size and composition of the sample size interviewed, on the observations relating to the functioning of Heaven and on the recommendations.

There is a wide debate among the gods about the need for a Chief Executive Officer. There is a general belief that this will only add a layer between God and gods and may not be in the best interests of Heaven and its speedy and efficient functioning. In fact R&D have pointed out that Hell works better because of a unison of command and, with no multiple power centres, decision making is quick as would exist in a dictatorship. While a benevolent dictatorship would be desirable in Heaven, everyone is aware that God himself is totally against such an administrative structure, and a CEO being a benevolent dictator may lead to heartburning among other gods.

One of the gods suggests that there be a revolving CEO, thereby giving all the gods a chance to be a CEO by turn. However there is no unanimity on this issue. After extensive debate the gods come to the conclusion that appointing a CEO may be a wiser option. Why not give it a try. If it does not work, the revolving CEO concept could be an acceptable option. At least with a CEO in place, the gods can leave all mundane administrative matters to the CEO. Moreover the CEO will be answerable to God for any failures or shortcomings. Though there is no unanimity on the appointment of a CEO who could give a direction and coordinate and oversee operations and give a direction to activity there is a reluctant acceptance that it's an option that may be tried out. It is also agreed that since this would be a fulltime job it may be better to source a competent CEO from earth who brings in some new perspectives.

Gandhi disagrees with the rest but overrules himself given the majority view.

It is agreed with no particular enthusiasm but with an attitude of resignation to appoint a CEO and St Peter is mandated to find a suitable candidate.

St Peter states that God is agreeable to experimentation with a CEO to conduct the day-to-day affairs of Heaven. He would however prefer the CEO to report to the All Souls'

Council rather than to God. Gandhi disagrees and would like the CEO to report to God. St Peter agrees to follow up.

It is generally agreed that the CEO should apply his mind to the recommendations made by R&D and implement these in consultation with God.

***

The Appointment of a CEO

'For Heaven's sake we need a CEO in Heaven,' says St Peter to Yamraj, the god of death. 'And we need one soon. Yamraj can you please put a Hoogle alert on all CEOs or persons with CEO-like abilities who are about to die and also do a Hoogle analytics on their chances of being admitted to Heaven? We could perhaps try headhunting through that consultancy firm, R&D. They provide these services but can only give us living CEOs on loan, short term or long term. We though need a dead CEO on a non-returnable basis. One, whose soul can be transported to Heaven and qualifies to live here. Not one wanting to go back to earth or qualifies only for Hell. These days there seems to be no commitment except to the green buck. When I tell earthlings that there is no such thing as money in Heaven, they just turn their backs. Now, why in God's name would anyone want money? We are providing them with everything. Everything.'

R&D is asked to shortlist and recommend CEO candidates for consideration to the newly proposed post. R&D's headhunting division gets to work. No celebrity CEO is willing to consider the position in a company that is not listed and will not offer stock options, joining bonuses, exit handshakes and tenure securities. A few non-celebrity CEO candidates, who are shortlisted based on their outstanding performances in their companies and are generally considered as star performers by industry observers, are sounded for a career move. All of them turn down the offer when told that it would be a one-way visit with no return options to earth. The suggestion that they would receive much better perks and privileges, a large mansion to live in and unlimited travel in space and time does not impress any of the potential candidates. R&D is embarrassed that it has failed in finding a potential candidate for a prestigious client, more so as it has never failed to hunt a head for any senior position in the past. R&D is worried about losing the massive commission promised for the placement plus the loss of face. St Peter keeps reminding R&D about the urgency to find a suitable person. R&D assures St Peter that they are very close to finding a candidate while expressing concern that the biggest hurdle has been to find one willing to leave earth. St Peter interprets this as confirmation of the declining popularity of Heaven.

Luckily for R&D, General Mart, one of the world's largest retail chain, and a Fortune 100 Company, goes into bankruptcy post allegations of fraud and mismanagement by the chairman and CEO of the company. Investigations into the financial mismanagement of the firm are ordered by the Federal agencies after several allegations are made by stockholders of the company accusing the CEO and the chairman, Marc Vanderschmidt, of perpetuating fraud, embezzlement of funds, nepotism in grant of contracts and a cover-up operation by misreporting financial statements, all of which have eroded the share value of the company enormously. Now Vanderschmidt is depressed by rumours of his imminent arrest. Vanderschmidt, who is unable to face the employee fury, the shareholder annoyance, the media reports about his focus on expensive wines, women and lavish lifestyle including private jets, luxury yachts and celebrity parties at the cost of the company, is no longer able to face his friends and family. All his bank accounts are frozen and his children are upset with their college mates passing snide remarks about their father. In desperation, Vanderschmidt attempts suicide. Unfortunately for him, he is rushed into emergency and the overdose of barbiturates is removed from his system and its effects nullified just in time to save his life after a near-death experience.

Yamraj gets a Hoogle alert the moment Vanderschmidt attempts suicide. Yamraj does a search. Yes, he is frustrated, has lost shareholder confidence and is likely to be sacked. He can't raise funds to keep the company going and has been hiding the fact that the company isn't doing too well by window dressing the company financials. Otherwise he seems to be God fearing and has been attending church fairly regularly. He has been divorced twice. Currently he is having an affair with a married woman who is insisting on a pre-nuptial that is bothering him. He has four children from the two earlier wives and one from an affair, though the adulteress pretends the child is her husband's. His professional career seems good. He has a lot of awards to his credit, citations, etc., from all sorts of organizations hailing him as the business leader, CEO of the year. Yamraj informs Peter and asks him if Vanderschmidt would qualify to enter Heaven.

'Hmmmm. I really don't know,' says Peter. 'It's getting increasingly difficult to find men of substance. Of course, we do not go by all those earthly morals, laws and social norms. His awards and peer group endorsements do not count. Anyone who has meaningfully contributed to improving life on earth alone will do. Maybe you should talk to this guy. Find out if he would be willing to die, which you believe he does, and offer himself as a candidate for the post of CEO in case he is selected. If he agrees bring him to the Judgement Hall. We will see if he passes muster.'

R&D is alerted by St Peter about a Hoogle search that has thrown up the name of Vanderschmidt.

Ronald tells St Peter that they have independently tracked Vanderschmidt as a potential candidate and hopes that this will ensure that R&D do not lose any consultancy fees with Heaven Inc claiming that the lead came from St Peter.

The attempted suicide is splashed all over the media although the company PR and Vanderschmidt's spokesperson maintain that it was an accidental overdose of medication.

R&D approaches Vanderschmidt at the hospital a day post his regaining consciousness. R&D have been consultants and auditors for General Mart and have known Vanderschmidt, and have even helped him by allowing him to report incomplete or half baked information or have overlooked information so that Vanderschmidt could have a smooth ride reporting the large profits that never existed, thereby artificially hiking up the share price of the company at Wall Street.

R&D offers Vanderschmidt a way out of the mess. They know that the solution will also help R&D get out of a messy situation as they did not qualify the audit reports and ended up misleading the shareholders. With Vanderschmidt dead they can claim before the Fed authorities that they had kept Vanderschmidt informed of inaccuracies and shift the blame onto him.

They offer Vanderschmidt a deal he cannot refuse: agree to die and take over in Heaven as the CEO or live on earth and face criminal charges, appear before Congress Committees and confront class action.

Vanderschmidt, fearing public shaming and isolation, agrees to the Heaven option as in any case he was planning to die but his attempt at suicide had failed. The deal offered assures a significant position and a place in Heaven, which he otherwise could not have hoped for. R&D also commit to using his death to create a sympathy wave for him and blame the Fed authorities for hounding a star performer to his grave. This way he could also salvage his reputation on earth and thereby have the best of both worlds.

Vanderschmidt arrives at the gates of Heaven, where he is met by St Peter. When he is presented before the Judges on the day of Judgement he is found unfit for Heaven. Now there is a serious problem. R&D communicate with St Peter and he is informed that after a very prolonged search they have found a CEO willing to take up the responsibility. They indicate that Vanderschmidt has won innumerable awards and has been the *Time* magazine's cover face of the year only a few years earlier. St Peter states that all of these do not matter in Heaven and count for zilch. He has been found unfit and will be sent to Hell.

R&D state that it would be extremely difficult to find another candidate and other candidates may be even worse. Vanderschmidt had agreed to their terms and now it would be very unfair to send him to Hell. He cannot even return to earth. R&D also indicate that Vanderschmidt if lost to Heaven may end up using his managerial skills in Hell and may even be vindictive since he is not being admitted to Heaven. Moreover Vanderschmidt is recognized as a true marketing genius. He took General Mart from a 2 billion dollar company to a 75 billion dollar company in a decade and created GENMAR which has the best brand recognition and recall value. He could certainly do the same for Heaven.

'We just need to give him a chance,' urges Ronald.

St Peter agrees to plead with the Judges. It is the first time he has pleaded for any soul. After a lot of discussion the Judges agree to give Vanderschmidt conditional entry into Heaven. He would get a one-year contract to prove his mettle. If within a year Heaven does not see a turnaround, where the market share of Heaven starts improving, Vanderschmidt goes to Hell. The Judges also wonder how a person who is otherwise unfit to enter Heaven can be deemed appropriate to run the place. St Peter argues that the compromise is for a valid reason and in any case for a limited trial period. He agrees to all the terms set forth by the Judges.

Vanderschmidt takes charge as the CEO and learns from St Peter about all the processes and procedures. He is also introduced to several key functionaries of Heaven. He is shocked to learn that there is no written constitution in Heaven. There are no laws, no law enforcement agencies, no prescribed rules and regulations. He is happy to learn that there is no Regulatory Authority to check company operations and dealings. Vanderschmidt studies the report of R&D. He is soon convinced that Heaven could be a great place to be in.

Vanderschmidt starts work on his vision of what Heaven should be. His hypothesis is based on the survival needs of humans and conflicts related thereto, or arising therefrom, being the key motivational drivers for human beings. Heaven has been structured so that survival needs are done away with. Conflicts also do not exist because of high entry restrictions clubbed with unlimited resources. Heaven's focus has been on allowing time, freedom and resources for the mind to develop creatively, improve self and environment and suggest ways and means to gods and God to improve life on earth and in other galaxies. While these have been laudable aims and goals, the security and comfort offered as also the lack of conflict has taken away the basic motivations to develop and grow.

In one of the discussions with St Peter, Vanderschmidt emphasizes that he would strongly recommend a change in the governing laws of Heaven. He would like insecurity and conflict to become a part of Heaven's governing mechanism where the goal of each soul can be to want to become a god or even God and get almost unlimited powers enjoyed by the gods. The conflict, ambition and struggle will lead to outputs that would be very valuable for the growth of the universe. In fact, depending on the competence of each soul, territories and galaxies can be carved out that could be ruled by a soul and such a soul should be free to add through conquest, negotiation, treachery or other means, good or bad, so as to expand its sphere of influence and increase its power. The status of gods can be conferred on a soul once the soul achieves an agreed critical power mass that can influence or compel others to surrender to his wishes. It would be a strategy similar to that on earth where kings and emperors ruled and controlled or CEOs and presidents increased their areas of influence and market shares of companies they managed. The competition among planetary systems, galaxies and beyond would lead to star wars that could output advanced technologies and value additions of a level unprecedented in galactical terms. The increasing powers of the gods will in itself enhance the status of God and increase his own power base.

He also propounds his theory on admissibility to Heaven. He is of the view that Heaven must admit people that can meaningfully contribute needed skill sets for growth. Heaven's current policy is very heavily skewed in favour of value system. This is resulting in some very specialized and key resource personnel being lost to Hell. The policy in Heaven needs to be designed along lines of an immigration policy such as in the US. Those who cannot contribute meaningfully and particularly in economic terms are kept out. Immigrants are kept out of areas where skill sets are adequately available locally. They are admiteed only in areas where skill sets are needed for spurring economic growth. A similar scheme in Heaven will ensure better screening than the current scheme. Effectiveness of the person should be the critical determining factor. Values do not necessarily translate into effectiveness. In fact those who are aggressive and ruthless are far more effective.

Vanderschmidt presents his white paper on Heaven which consists of a Memorandum and Articles of Association, a Vision statement, a Mission statement, a ten year plan, goals and targets, job responsibilities, reward and punishment, incentive schemes and MIS. He is mighty pleased with his task as none of these documents ever existed or were created in Heaven and he is expecting a good pat on the back in a personal meeting with God.

Finally the day arrives when Vanderschmidt meets God. He is very excited and makes a presentation to God, trying not to feel overawed.

God expresses total disappointment with Vanderschmidt's vision and thought flow. God states that Vanderschmidt's entire thinking is an earth-influenced thought process. One that lacks creativity and is not based on sound value-based principles. God's creation of Heaven is in order to have a place where souls reap a reward for what they have achieved or how they conducted themselves on earth. Heaven is not the place to prove and consolidate, it is meant to be the place to enjoy the fruits, post a meaningful and value-led struggle on earth. On earth the pursuit was all the time after goals set by others. Yes, there may be some advantages in the way earthlings think. However, after seeing the way value systems have changed, God believes that it is perhaps not an ideal model. He certainly has no intentions of making Heaven another crucible for unsustainable growth.

'What is needed is a sustainable environment where the mind can be happy, free of fear, willing to experiment, thirsting to know the truth, hankering for knowledge and be at peace in a secure environment. Happiness in itself should be the goal. If such a mix did not produce the dynamics for growth or change, so be it. It cannot be a contention that to achieve wrong objectives we need to put in place a matching structure. Happiness is a state of the mind. In fact, those who have created for themselves that state on earth have created their own Heaven on earth. Unfortunately pleasure and happiness are mixed up. Yes, no doubt pleasure can lead to momentary happiness. But happiness is not a stimulus-related response as pleasure is, it is a state in which the mind is aware, alive, in control and at peace. Pleasure is turned off almost as soon as the stimulus is switched off. It should not be the intention of reintroducing in Heaven the same structure that leads to creating another earth here.

'Yes, Hell may have followed a structure that is an extension of earth, in fact from the view point of illusionary pleasure perhaps an even better zone than earth. This has no doubt helped Hell promote itself as a preferred destination for the souls, but pleasurable gratification is only one part of Hell. The price to pay is the loss of values, dignity and self respect, the absence of creative or innovative endeavours and the assignment of one's soul to Satan. It may be an easy solution as everything is offered on a platter and thereafter the soul is only living in an illusionary, non-real, simulated world without even the awareness of the complete loss of thinking capacity and freedom.

'You are because you think. You exist because you think. Any vision of Heaven therefore must ensure that it takes the soul way beyond its earthly body-confined existence. Its dwelling in the body is merely to assimilate the attributes, and post liberation from the body to use its newly acquired power of movement in space and time, of immortality, of unlimited access to resources to the advantage of understanding the growth, development and evolution of life and contribute meaningfully for its improvement.'

Vanderschmidt is impressed with God's explanation and does not know how to counter the argument with his own theory of aggrandizement. He has never met a chairman of a company with such clarity of thought and vision. He meekly states that he now comprehends God's vision and agrees to work to achieve the same. Vanderschmidt is about to thank God when he realizes that God is not there, there is just a vacuum where he perceived God just a moment earlier. He wonders if God was there at all or was it just an illusion and he was hearing an inner voice. He is unsure.

Vanderschmidt reflects on his own life in the light of what he believes God said and suddenly, he sees how meaningless his life was, how unimportant his achievements were, how hollow the applauds of his colleagues were, how insignificant the wealth he believed he created was. He realizes that he wasted his time on earth and pursued the wrong goals, barked up the wrong tree, and all along believed that he was doing something important.

He decides to change his own thought process and to change the way he lives. Just as his challenge on earth, in his earlier assignments, was to stay ahead of the changes in the external business environment, his challenge now is to ensure a paradigm shift in his own thought process and vision.

Vanderschmidt now gets down to organize his office and to put his organizational skills to create better communication and enjoy the moment-related activity rather than target-related activity. Vanderschmidt realizes that the concept of time frames and working towards deadlines is virtually non-existent in Heaven. It is clear that when time is infinite and souls are immortal there is no need to hurry up anything. The activity pace should be one that allows the performer to savour the moment, be relaxed and at peace. Vanderschmidt realizes that in the absence of any compulsion to perform, lack of any monetary incentives and absence of any time lines, his tools of enforcing corporate discipline in Heaven are virtually non-existent. He has to come out with solutions that are congruent with a different operating framework of Heaven with its far more democratic and relaxed functioning. He realizes that the objectives of Heaven are not to reach any goals or to outsmart competition, or to beef up bottom lines and ensure top line growth, or to submit quarterly performance reports. The idea is really to treat the journey itself as a goal, to encourage and even assist competition, to focus on quality, governance standards, best practices and to enjoy the process. End results are of no consequence or importance. There are no rewards or punishments waiting. There are no auditors to answer to and no shareholders to please.

A thought passes his mind: if only there had been no punishments on earth he could have got away with all his decisions that had led to enormous profits and massive bonus cheques. He believes what he did on earth were standard industry accepted accounting policies and in fact he had been highly creative and even ingenious in devising shell companies to show transactions that helped shore up company profits and profitabilities. He was hoping that in Heaven his creativity would be recognized and appreciated. In the absence of any monetization in Heaven there is no question of accounting reports or profits or bonuses.

He realizes he is relapsing into earthly thought processes. He knows he needs to exorcise the ghosts of earth. The Devil has been active in his mind on earth and his presence is still there even though he is in Heaven. He cannot let the Devil dominate him here in Heaven. He is convinced by God of the bigger, better design that he had missed. He now has to get a grip over himself and do the right thing. It is payback time. He has been given a new chance.

As he sits down to think of new strategies he is left wondering how he would devise methods to motivate all souls to act towards a purpose.

He sets out to first define a Vision and Mission statement in the light of God's reaction to his earth conditioning.

The draft New Vision statement:

To provide all souls an equal opportunity to enter Heaven through a transparent and fair evaluation process based on their demonstrated value contribution on earth and to ensure a gainful, meaningful, peaceful, interactive and adventurous post life in Heaven rewarded with pleasure, joy, happiness in a friendly environment that encourages improvement and application of talent in Heaven to better life around galaxies, guiding the evolutionary process in a way that would over time negate the shortcomings seen on earth and elsewhere in the universe.

The Mission statement:

1. To evolve and improve infrastructure in communication and transmovement such that post life is better understood on earth and life itself is better led on earth.
2. To put in place, a better response mechanism between the gods in Heaven and the earthlings wishing to relate with them while emphasizing that people have to help themselves and not look skyward for help.
3. To better understand the evolutionary process, remove dependency on godly intervention, understand the values respected in Heaven.

Vanderschmidt now works on his most critical problem. The connect with clients. It is what he has been advocating and focusing on in all the companies he has headed. It is his key to success. 'You service clients by connecting with them, understanding them and their needs and efficiently fulfilling these needs.' Many of his books on business management in large enterprises had focused on his theories of client connect. Now he is dealing with the largest corporation he has ever dealt with. He still likes to perceive Heaven Inc. as a corporation and would like to ensure changes that make Heaven a desirable place for an unending holiday. He now has to establish the working of his theories in the new environment, in an environment that is not driven by greed and ambition; one that is not oiled by the lure of big bucks, one where reward and punishment or pleasure and fear are not the driving force. He decides that if there is to be a connect with the clients, it must begin with a response to prayers.

There are billions of people out there praying each night. Clients who are trying to reach out to a corporation indicating their needs. The belief is very strong that this corporation can indeed fulfil their needs, that the corporation is headed by none other than God who can at a snap of His fingers do whatever He likes. The fact that Heaven is rarely responding has not been a deterrent to the clients. Their belief that one must pray hard and long enough to be heard seems well entrenched. Clients are even willing to blame themselves if prayers are not answered.

This seems to Vanderschmidt to be a good starting point.

He is certain that if he can crack the problem of a better response mechanism God would be pleased. On earth he would have introduced a highly efficient mechanism to respond to such a huge demand and would have fulfilled them at a price payable by the client ensuring a healthy top line and a very attractive bottom line. In Heaven though after what God has told him, he knows he cannot link response to payment. How do you run a charity organization where the client pays nothing, yet you go on fulfilling their demands. He banks on the fact that Heaven has unlimited resources. He decides to take the first step by implementing one of R&D's recommendations. Put in place a 1-800-PRAYERS number with a huge automated call centre.

Vanderschmidt calls in his IT experts and puts a team in place headed by Doraiswamy. The mandate to the team is clear. All prayers must be processed at top speed, categorized suitably and responses ensured.

The mandate is clear but the task is highly complex. The team works on the task for several weeks, puts together a sophisticated algorithm to deal with the very large volumes and very varied demands. Finally they are ready to make a presentation to Vanderschmidt to let him know the magnitude of the problem.

Doraiswamy admits that in his estimate earthlings are moving away from God as the perception among earthlings is that their prayers are not being heard or answered.

The logistics of collecting, translating, collating, analyzing, retrieving, understanding, archiving prayers is enormous. The transactions run into trillions of units every day. Despite the best of computing power and a large battery of minds working on them 24/7 there are problems. The 1-800-PRAYER line in Beta testing is not very popular. This is an automated system that processes the transaction and auto responds reducing the burden on the centralized system. The system of acknowledging receipt of the prayer can be problematic as this only leads to greater expectations and more heartburns in case of no responses.

Vanderschmidt says he thought the new high tech call centre set up had resolved the issue.

Doraiswamy says there are a lot of glitches. He says problems vary from language issues, time zone issues, unreasonable demands in prayers and offers a live demo to

Vanderschmidt. He dials the 1-800-PRAYER and a pleasant heavenly voice responds.

'Thank you for saying your prayers. Your prayers are important to us and we will be with you as soon as a god is free to attend. While you are holding on please press 1 to hear Bhajans, 2 to hear recitations from Koran, 3 to hear Psalms from the Bible, 4 to...'

Vanderschmidt is surprised.

'...We have not received any response, please press 1 if you are a Hindu, 2 if you are a Muslim, 3 if you are a Catholic, 4 if you are a Buddhist, 5 if you are a Jew, 6 if you are a Jain, 7 if you are a protestant, 8 if you...'

Vanderschmidt presses 1 to test it out.

'If you are a Shiv bhakta press 1, if a Ram devotee press 2, if you pray to Ganesha press 3, if to Hanuman press 4, if to Vishnu press 5...' (Vanderschmidt is now holding the phone for quite some time)... 'if to Saraswati press 286...'

'You see,' says Doraiswamy, 'why we are not ready to use this system.'

He further adds, 'While we are recording the prayers we are not able to process them fast enough. Currently it is taking years to respond to prayers, and the faith of people is being eroded. We need more staff to increase the speed of processing. The average age of earthlings in Heaven is over 65 even if they live in younger bodies. They are slow at their responses. Many are not net or computer savvy, are making frequent mistakes and get bored very soon. The younger earthlings seem to end up in Hell. The younger lot is net savvy, hence Hell has a much better IT system and a much more efficient response mechanism. In fact, much to our embarrassment, when we had a server crash the engineers from Hell offered to rectify the problem and even suggested we outsource the maintenance and upgradation of Heaven's IT system to them. Of course, for security reasons we declined. Imagine if the Devil was to learn about all prayers voicemailed to God.

'The problem about processing,' continues Doraiswamy, 'is that the prayers generally relate to health, wealth and success. These are issues to be resolved by the executives not the IT. Instructions on such matters are that there is to be no interference with natural laws. Laws of the universe and evolution, laws of the battle for survival must be allowed to prevail on earth as that is what was envisaged by nature. Interference by way of miracles or divine intervention, is not permissible. How then do you respond to prayers? One option is that we let earthlings know that there will be no responses to prayers. Let them know that they must help themselves. That would also be in line with God's own desire and the new Mission statement.'

'I understand,' says Vanderschmidt. 'Only it may further alienate the earthlings. Let me think over the issue to find the appropriate solution.' Vanderschmidt has a sinking feeling that the IT plans which he had hoped to demonstrate to God as a major achievement are now falling to bits. He knows that the task on hand is one that only God can resolve but God refuses to do so as that is against the laws of nature. Shouldn't the law of God supersede the laws of nature, he wonders?

***

God's Visit to Hell

The gods reassemble to discuss the implementation of R&D's recommendations. Vanderschmidt makes a presentation indicating how he proposes to implement the recommendations.

Vanderschmidt indicates that the R&D report covers three major segments of recommendations. The first is about redefining the Mission and Vision statement of Heaven and ensuring a marketing campaign on earth that enables the right communication to people about the purpose of Heaven, what earthlings can expect in Heaven, and why Heaven is a superior choice over Hell. The marketing campaign is not to be handled through the traditional marketeers such as religious leaders, rituals or gospels but through modes used and understood by people including social media such as Facebook, Whatsapp, Instagram, Twitter, YouTube and many more. The communication has to be directly sent after appropriate TG research by the Heaven research cell supported by R&D's own team. The communication must promote interactivity. Vanderschmidt indicates that he has already prepared the Mission and Vision statements and needs their collective approval. A whole new campaign is being prepared. He will build in an interactive mechanism so that there is continuous feedback and midstream correction possible. He will ensure that the attributes and USP of the product being marketed are emphasized and once again the souls are attracted to what used to be a strong brand. He hopes not only to regain the market share but also increase the market share and regain the dominant market leadership. The reasons for the brand dilution have been studied and he is taking steps to reposition brand Heaven in a way that the past glory can be regained.

The second part is about restructuring the functioning in Heaven by regrouping departments, specifying activities and timeframes and working more cohesively with the help of the CEO's office to ensure that duplicity and confusion is avoided. This would require several gods to give up or at least not exercise powers they possess, and leave it to the appropriate designated skilled and empowered god to deal with sectorial needs. This would build efficiencies and enhance effectiveness. It would bring about discipline in action, it would ensure better coordination and superior delivery thereby re-establishing Heaven's image in the marketplace. Vanderschmidt would like to propose an organisational structure that would allow enough flexibility while avoiding working in silos yet ensuring that responsibilities are fairly well defined. Reporting structures and management information systems would be immediate and such that they facilitate better internal communication and coordination and help develop synergies between departments. This would also unlock a lot of non-performing assets and speed up deliverables.

The third segment is on supporting infrastructure and systems. Here the idea is to introduce motivation through a reward system. Introduction of IT systems that help better and speedier communication with the right TG through Hoogle analytics would help ensure superior back office support.

Issues are raised by some of the gods present on hurdles in implementation, concern about endless trolling if interactivity with Heaven and its denizens is introduced as trolls have become quite fashionable with earthlings given the palm-held democracy that technology has enabled, the response that can be expected from Hell to counter the new strategies of Heaven, the back up plan in case plan A fails, etc. Vanderschmidt expresses confidence in his plans but it is obvious that the same is not shared by others.

A question is raised on the conclusions drawn by R&D based on hearsay evidence with no conclusive evidence presented in relation to Hell or its functioning.

St Peter admits that this is a major flaw in the report.

All the gods are now very confused. They do not know what should be done next. They suggest God, who has all the answers, should tell them the solution.

God says that there is nothing wrong in people choosing Hell, and if Hell is indeed getting more attractive because the Devil is improving things there then that is a very healthy sign. One of the gods wonders if there is anyway they could find out what the Devil has done to improve the image and services of Hell. God says that the best course would be for St Peter to visit Hell in person since R&D was unable to do so.

St Peter protests saying that Lucifer and he worked together at one point in the past, but Lucifer was banished by God given his warped thinking and attitude. Lucifer always held Peter responsible for his excommunication and Lucifer believed it was owing to Peter misinforming God that he was banished from Heaven. Lucifer has never forgiven Peter ever since. Hence his visit to Hell would not be desirable given the prejudice that Lucifer holds against him. Lucifer may even cast his evil spell on him and influence him adversely. The only entity who can withstand the evil influence of Lucifer is God himself and he would be willing to accompany God to Hell to convince Lucifer to play fair, adopt good governance practices and not adopt malpractices to achieve his goals, but he would not dare to go alone.

All the gods look towards God.

God readily agrees to visit Lucifer in Hell.

Everyone is aghast at the thought of God visiting Lucifer's kingdom. Would Lucifer welcome God? Would he show Him due respect? Would his dealings with God be dignified? How would he respond to Peter?

God asks St Peter to plan a visit to Hell.

There is a lot of buzz in Heaven as God has never stepped into Hell although he has been traveling across galaxies. God in Hell is something no one could ever have dreamt of.

Not surprisingly when St Peter calls Lucifer through a thought-call, the Devil gleefully welcomes God's proposed visit and agrees to show God around Hell. The Devil tells St Peter that he has been waiting for this call. He was always sure that God would visit him one day. That moment has arrived. Now he can show God the power of Hell.

It will be God's first visit to Hell ever since Hell was created.

God arrives in Hell accompanied by Vanderschmidt and St Peter.

The fires of Hell are visible from far away. The night sky glows as if all the forests were on fire at the same time. In a strange way the lit up night sky looks beautiful. As there is no daylight in Hell this is the motif of Hell through time and space. God points out to Peter and Vanderschmidt, who are accompanying Him, the beauty of Hell seen in the distant sky. Peter and Vanderschmidt are not impressed. They are in fact quite worried and nervous.

As they reach Hell a huge imposing gate opens. A glowing sign in the sky above the gate of Hell reads: 'Halt! You are entering the Kingdom of Lucifer!'

Lucifer's lieutenants receive God at the gates of Hell and bow in courtesy. They escort God to Lucifer on a chariot of gold. Smartly turned out security guards march on both sides of the chariot in perfect unision. The passage is full of decorations made from human skulls and bones. Radiating light dazzles in spurts emphasizing the power of the Devil. There are neon lights, lasers, tasers and electronic signboards screaming the virtues of Hell, promising youth and worldly pleasures with no limits, no values, no tomorrows. It all looks very impressive. The Halls they pass through are all large, dimly lit, with discotheque decor and surreal paintings similar to works of Dali but much more grotesque.

As they reach the Hall of the Mighty at the end of the long corridor, Lucifer is seen sitting on his throne made of human bones. Lucifer welcomes God in his royal chamber. It looks like a huge house of horror with bats, lizards and snakes crawling all over. St Peter and Vanderschmidt seem very uncomfortable in the environment. Lucifer guides God into a sette that is obviously smaller than his own. St Peter and Vanderschmidt are shown to their chairs beside God.

St Peter is offended that God is seated on a small sette, while the royal throne is occupied by Lucifer, but God seems unperturbed and totally at ease. All of Lucifer's cronies are standing around Lucifer with their horns glowing and tails gently wagging.

God thanks Lucifer for his hospitality and for welcoming them to Hell.

Lucifer ignores St Peter and Vanderschmidt and says he has been waiting for this day for eons. He knew one day God would condescend to come down to him, to Hell—his empire which he is proud of.

God introduces Vanderschmidt and St Peter to Lucifer. Lucifer nods as if indicating that he knows them both but does not think much of them.

God congratulates Lucifer on his empire, his aggressive marketing techniques and his strategies to attract earthlings.

Lucifer says that he knows why God is here. He knows about the R&D report. Success lies in selling what you want while making the earthlings believe that that is exactly what they want. The packaging is important he states.

Before God can tell Lucifer that he has been adopting unfair means, Lucifer, as if anticipating such an allegation, counter complains to God about the misinformation being spread about Hell to the earthlings by God's religious emissaries. He cites the example of the earthlings being told that Hell is all fire.

'That is just not true as can be seen,' says Lucifer. 'We only have fire as a prop to lighten up the night sky, to flag our presence, but inside here it is cool and comfortable. Yes, there are a few fire chambers to be used when people need to be disciplined. Otherwise we allow them all the freedom they want, except the freedom of speech and free thought. These freedoms are of no use to hell mates. Their focus is on physical pleasures and Hell provides enough of that to keep them happy. After all, what does it take to provide physical pleasures; just loud music, strobing lights, strong visuals, alcohol, drugs, virtual and augmented reality sequences. Just like in a video game inmates here can create or follow whatever moments they desire. In any case, of what use is freedom? I can think for them and I know what's best for them.'

'Lucifer, you know that's not true. Heaven does not indulge in such false campaigns,' says St Peter. 'Yes, Heaven may have failed to market itself to earthlings, but we have not indulged in deriding Hell or spreading false propaganda.'

Lucifer interjects, 'Not only do I have a better product to offer, I also have a better marketing strategy. Addressed to the right target group. You market Heaven to the ageing for they are at the right age for transiting to the new world. But you are wrong. Marketing is all about entering the mind space when the mind is impressionable. I target the youth. I invest in them over a longer period of time. I am not seeking immediate results or gains. But once I have captured their mind space I have them by the hook. I can get them whenever I want. The youth are looking for worldly pleasures, for immediate gratification, for physical stimulus, for sex. They are not looking for all those silly things you offer in Heaven.'

'I am impressed with your marketing. I can see the results,' adds God. 'Heaven believes that mankind should have a choice. It should know what that choice is and what the implications are, in the short term and in the long term. It should have a free mind to choose correctly. And it should be prepared and have imbibed the values to be worthy of the option chosen. You create your own Heaven or Hell on earth and then you choose to transit to the same comfort zone. One must however not miss the product for the packaging. You have packaged very well. There is no denying that. Maybe Heaven has failed to market the virtues of the product.'

'Virtues are not what earthlings are looking for. These are all outdated concepts. The new generation is the now generation. They want all their worldly pleasures and they want them now. Not wait to get the promised glories and joys when they move to the Promised Land. I allow them pleasures now. Whatever they want. There are no restrictions. Live for today. And if you die you will be in Hell where all those worldly pleasures and more will continue. Yes, in return I ask for their soul. Is that a high price? You see here in Hell all the souls are mine. Mine alone. They belong to me. They obey me. They do just what I want. Their bodies do not rot in Hell as propagated. Their bodies are left behind on earth to rot six feet under. Here they live in an illusionary world. They continue to enjoy the pleasures of the world in this illusionary world. They don't need to live in reality. Their reality ends on earth. It is my master stroke. You however carry on with a new reality in Heaven, or at least that is the illusion you create for them, making them believe that they are living a reality.'

Lucifer continues, 'I have eliminated all real contact between people. All contacts are only virtual. However the earthlings do not know that these are only virtual. They don't really care. In any case, the now generation lives their life on earth in virtual space, through social media. Here at least they believe the virtual is real. It's how it should be. You can control minds better by making people believe what they would like to believe. If sound levels and other stimuli are high, the souls are not able to hear their own inner thoughts that may mislead them. It's best that the souls are drowned in extraneous noises and stimuli. If you speak to them, most inmates will tell you how satisfied they are. Why don't I take you around so you can see for yourself.

'Peter, Vander, I am sure you would like to join the tour as well. You can't go back not having seen the wonders of Hell. You will be the privileged ones who can talk about Hell to others.'

Lucifer takes God along with St Peter and Vanderschmidt on a conducted tour of Hell and shows them the IT centre, the master server farm, the communication lines, the fright chambers (he avoids showing the torture chambers and the violence rooms), the virtual reality labs, the Hi-tech centre, the health clubs, the floating mobility transportation systems, the space-time control systems, the floating and wandering bodies Air Traffic Control systems, the soul reorientation centre, the body-soul separating and fusing centre, the master control room, the recreation centres, the physical pleasure zones, the gambling centres, the gaming zones, the winner takes all free for all centres, and other locations.

The work culture in Hell seems to be one of high motivation. Satan does not miss out on the opportunity to point this out to God. God smiles as if in acknowledgement. Money seems to be the motivator. Satan has obviously seen the advantage of retaining a monetary system and has exploited it to the hilt. He has encouraged greed. It is clear that all those entering Hell are made aware of the fact that all goods and services are to be paid for.

'Nothing is free. Everything can be purchased for a price. Greed is good. There are no rules and regulations except that the Devil must be obeyed. Since souls entering Hell carry no money, they are given doles based on the level of information they provide on their near and dear ones. Information that Hell's marketing team can use to its advantage while influencing, entrapping and controlling the mind. For the greed of money Hellers are willing to sell information about their friends, their lovers and their relatives. The lesson in treachery extends to each one using any and all tools to build their financial strengths. Money can be hoarded in banks and used to bargain for positions that offer rewards, which in turn helps to earn more money. Money can be used to pay for all goods and services; to enter night clubs, buy drugs, or even bribe a prisoner. Money can be used to buy love, pay for sex or slaves and even to purchase peace. There is no restriction on making money as long as the taxes due to the Devil are paid. Money is taxed at undefined rates and transferred to the Devil's account with no questions asked. Those who have no money are condemned to work and slog it out in the fires of Hell. Everyone is busy. Time is money. If you do not cheat, the other guy will cheat you. Things like friendship, trust, love or care are absent in Hell. But this is not visible to an unsuspecting visitor. Hell is a well-oiled machinery with highly motivated souls chasing inexplicable wealth dreams.'

'Thank you, Lucifer, for the courtesy extended to us,' offers Vanderschmidt. 'We have learnt a lot from this visit. You have a standing invitation of returning to Heaven either for a visit or to join back the team and dissolve Hell. What do you think of a merger of Heaven and Hell, Peter?'

Peter is shocked at Vanderschmidt's suggestion. He is uncertain if it is a serious statement or meant as a joke. He looks towards God who is nonchalant.

'I thought you were the one trying to figure out how to restructure Heaven,' retorts Lucifer. 'You are the one who appointed those consultants to help restructure. I need no rethink. I know I am doing a great job and I have the results to prove it. I surely have my competitors worried, haha. And please don't restructure Heaven on the basis of the R&D report.'

'Oh you know about the R&D report,' asks St Peter somewhat surprised.

'Yes, of course. That guy Ronald who wrote the report—he died last week. In a car crash! A new Ferrari purchased with the money you paid him, Peter. He was drunk. He was celebrating his wealth that night. But that is not important. What is, is that after his death he opted for Hell. This guy Ronald, who advised you on how Heaven should operate, ended up in Hell. With me! Now how do you answer that! He told me all about the report. He even told me that a lot of the report was cooked up, for they had no access to Hell or Heaven. Their report was made up based on all the insight you gave them about Heaven and some so-called research asking a few thousand silly earthlings about their views. People always answer questions to please the questioner. They rarely tell the truth. They made up what they thought Hell would be like. About Heaven their only source was you, Peter. So, Peter, all that is reported about Heaven is only one man's, sorry one angel's, point of view.

'If you have the time and inclination I could reintroduce you to Ronald!' chuckles Lucifer.

No one responds. God is unimpressed but listens to Lucifer. His smile clearly indicates he can see more than the Devil would like him to see. St Peter is very impressed and worried as well. He does not know what to make of Ronald's presence in Hell or the R&D report. Vanderschmidt is impressed with all that he has seen and wishes he had such powers on earth where he did not need to answer to Federal agencies and where he could implement his plans without restrictions. He could have built the world's largest corporation, created enormous wealth for the shareholders, and himself become the richest man on earth. If only he could have similar powers in heaven.

He has never seen any organized group of people with such high levels of motivation as he has seen in Hell. He is convinced that fear of authority and monetary greed is what makes Hell work with clockwork precision and efficiency. The same model could work in Heaven but how can he convince God, who has a totally different perspective, to adopt the model in Hell. The dollar may not be a bad currency to introduce in Heaven, he thinks. After having seen the efficient functioning of Hell, he is certain that God will not object to the introduction of a monetary system in Heaven. He could certainly do with some bankers in Heaven.

At the end of the visit God thanks Lucifer for showing Him around, praises the well-organized set-up with well-assigned responsibilities and Lucifer's own management skills.

God confesses that things seem to be working more efficiently in Hell than in Heaven, though He is uncertain if He would go the Hell route and place emphasis on form rather than content. He would never put restrictions on free thought or free speech, for that is the most important and necessary attribute for a happy being. Lucifer believes and tells God that He is living in a fool's paradise. People want to be served everything on a platter. They don't want to think or take decisions. God is wasting his time. He has all the resources at his command to drive things the way he would like them, but instead God has chosen a laissez faire policy and allowed life to evolve. 'Evolution is not desirable', says Lucifer. 'Creation is needed. Create things the way you want. Create life as you would like it. Don't allow it to evolve. Control and Command! Make sure nothing moves without your approval. Every event must be as per your order.'

God responds that He is happy the way evolution works and will have it no other way. Lucifer's policies can only yield short term gains, they are not policies on which a strong, long, lasting empire can be built where people live in love, happiness and joy.

Lucifer smiles and retorts that the reality is that it is his empire that is growing.

'You finally see my kingdom. I knew you would someday want to come and see for yourself what your fallen angel has created. Your angels may shout themselves hoarse about how terrible this place is. But what do they know. None of them have visited this place,' Lucifer looks mischievously at St Peter, 'except St Peter, now finally. And you can see for yourself how wonderful Hell is. How ill-informed your angels are. How misinformed your campaign about Hell is.'

'You were one of my most trusted angels, one of the best,' says God.

'I was the best. Yet you banished me from Heaven.'

'Yes, you were the best. But I never banished you from Heaven. You chose to move out. You wanted to be the ultimate ruler, the Almighty of your kingdom, and you said if it could not be the one in Heaven, you would create your own kingdom. You went out and created your kingdom. You chose this place called Hell and made it what it is today. I am considered the architect of Heaven and Hell, but my only contribution to the creation of Hell was not stopping you from creating one. I am open to experimentation and what you were doing was an experiment. It wasn't something I would do, but it wasn't something I would stop you from doing either.'

'Can we have this discussion in private,' suggests Lucifer.

God and Lucifer move into Lucifer's private chambers.

Lucifer continues, 'You have been very unfair in throwing me out of Heaven but now you can see for yourself what has been achieved by me despite all odds. You have appointed this Vanderschmidt as your CEO in Heaven. Ha. I would not have given him any responsibility if he was to come to Hell which I am sure he would have, had it not been for the favours shown by St Peter. You talk of principles and values but you break these to appoint cheaters on earth as CEO. Look at the record of some of your emissaries. Rapists, pedophiles, mass murderers, destroyers! They ruined the earth, created an environment for brother to turn against brother and are now in safe refuge in Heaven, thanks to you.

'I was running Heaven for you. I would have taken Heaven places. And you would not have had competition from me. Only you did not agree with my vision. You threw me out. I am now CEO of Hell and see the results. You need to be a CEO yourself. Not delegate this responsibility to gods or some incompetent earthling. The way to run a company is like a private limited company, not like a listed public company responsible to shareholders. You have given undue powers to the souls in Heaven. You have given them equal ownership. What for? What have they done to earn this reward? You have gone even further. You run the place like a charitable foundation with all stakeholders having equal ownership. It's little wonder that no one listens to you any longer. No one believes in you or your leadership. Don't be taken in by all those praying to you. It is only to get favours out of you. Not because they love you. You need to run the place with a whiplash, determining and changing rules that suit you. Be the ultimate decision maker. You have instead let evolutionary forces run the earth and then allowed similar scientific principles to run Heaven. You know the human mind is gullible. They will just follow any authoritarian leadership. You should have let me run the place for you, not let those incompetent satraps of yours do so. You have so many more important things to do around the universe.

You should stop wasting your time on this small, insignificant planet called earth. I have shown you the way. Let me run earth and Heaven for you. There's a lot more for you to do.'

'You know that you left Heaven of your own accord, Lucifer,' responds God. 'I never banished you from Heaven. That's a story you made up to give yourself a martyr's status. You had great ambitions and never believed in the goodness of the soul or the betterment of the soul.'

'Yes, I did opt out of Heaven. I, Lucifer, thought that so much more could be done with the soul. The soul, and even more its body, was so very manipulative because it followed the laws of chaos. Laws which were created by you! You created entropy. It was only natural that everything moved towards chaos. I only wanted to move that chaos in a direction that made sense to me. You then wanted chaos to be replaced by order. That implied reversing chaos in an environment that only moved towards greater entropy.'

'It was not the direction in which you wanted to see the chaos move,' adds God, 'it was your insatiable urge to control souls. It was about power over them. Everything had to happen the way you liked it. It was just the opposite of the way I believe it should be. As the all powerful I could have had everything the way I like it, yet I do not want it to be so. Though people believe that things work the way I desire, wish or decide, it is actually just the opposite. I would like them to make their choices. To determine the direction in which they would like to move. You exploited this principle and wanted things to move in the direction that you liked. You also realized that the soul could be influenced better if you had already influenced the body. The body was designed to react to external stimuli. That was a need for survival. That was a need of evolution. You exploited that principle by providing stimuli that teased the senses, provoked the senses and addicted them to these stimuli to the extent that their dependency on you increased. They now were dependent on this stimuli even after death, in their soul form, not knowing that such stimuli has no value in the afterlife. You used this as a marketing tool that provided promise but no delivery. You knew very well that once they entered your kingdom there would be no choice, no escape. It was all about creating the illusion on earth about the physical gratifications in Hell. I would have had no problems if you had been fair and honest in your pursuit of souls, but you broke the promise and pact and used unfair means to entice the soul.'

'You are aware that I worked hard to set up Heaven,' responds Lucifer, 'to give shape to your dream and vision, to provide an afterlife post the crucible of chaos on earth. You wanted intellectualism to prevail in Heaven and lead to experimentation and thoughts to create a better universe. I did not believe that we were achieving much that way. At least not in the time frames I would have preferred. I wanted immediate results and gratification. I wanted an extension of the chaos on earth even magnified if need be. I differed with you and therefore left to set up my own space. Hell was my creation, my vision even if you are credited for its creation. You see here what I have created. I have complete control over the souls. I can do what I like. I am God here. You call yourself God but you are less powerful than I am. You came to me. I did not come to you. I did not need to come to you. What you refer to as misleading marketing is really a highly successful campaign. What succeeds is what matters. Ethics and regulations are for fools. Now all souls want to come to Hell. That in itself is my victory. The fact that you have come down to Hell to meet with me is a sign of my success! Would you have come to me if these souls were not opting to come to me?'

'Lucifer, you know that I did not need to come down here to know what was happening. I am the omnipresent. I am the all knowing. If I had desired I could have destroyed Hell even without coming here. But you are aware that I will do no such thing. I would consider the defeat of evil forces through the use of force a defeat in itself. Evil has to be destroyed by good. That is why I am here. To talk reason to you! There may be easier options. But the option one must choose is the option which follows the right path, not the one that is easy.'

'Why are you so keen on my own little sphere of influence? There is a vast infinite universe that you created or brought into existence through forces of nature, as you claim, that you can control the way you want to but do not do. Why don't you take care of all of that? Why are you so concerned about a few souls in Hell? In any case, I like to believe that the souls like it here. They are here either out of choice or because Peter turned them away at the Pearly Gates of Heaven. Why shed tears for them now? And why show concern about how I treat them? If you really wanted to see them treated better you should have ensured that they were admitted into Heaven.'

'True. The fact of the matter however is that I want the souls to make an informed choice. The choice of Hell or Heaven is not made at the gates of Heaven or Hell. The choice is not made by Peter or Lucifer. It is made on earth. Each soul creates his or her own Hell or Heaven on earth. It has been my intention that we should help the earthlings in their effort to create their earthly Heaven and then transit to heavenly Heaven. I let them choose for themselves. I provided a conscience that guides them towards right and wrong. Unfortunately you have been tampering with the Heavenly plans. You are numbing the conscience. You are entering their bodies to brainwash them into believing that physical stimulus is all that life is about. You have been marketing Hell successfully, but wrongly and unethically. I have no problem with those choosing Hell, as long as their choice is not influenced, coerced or taken when they are brainwashed.'

'Oh come on,' retorts Lucifer. 'All is fair in love and war as they say. All is also fair in marketing campaigns. The most successful campaigns are rarely ethical. The brilliant ones are those that break all the rules of marketing and resort to disruptive or viral marketing. You control life all over the universe. You create new life. You determine the rules of creation or evolution. There are worlds out there with higher forms of life than earth, which are all under your control. I would like to enter that space. You need to open up these new markets and not have a monopolistic approach. I wish there was a competition commission. It would have easily put Heaven in its place for its anti trust measures. It would have brought better competitive spirit in the marketplace that could have been beneficial to the souls. You should seriously think in terms of opening up the rest of the universe to free market forces and put a regulatory commission in place rather than being a player and the regulator yourself.

'Why don't we just make a deal. You leave planet earth to me. You can keep Heaven for all other life forms. Let me deal with earthlings and their souls. How do a few hundred billion souls matter to you? You have gazillions of life forms and living creatures, many even superior to the earthlings. You focus on the rest of them. I will take care of all the souls in Hell. If I know I have hundred per cent of the market of human souls I do not need to resort to marketing campaigns or to tell lies. The earthlings will know their destiny. They may continue with their belief in God, in you. But they will worship me. And how does that matter to you? You are not egoistic. In any case you do not want people to believe in the supernatural. You are a rationalist. A super scientist let's say. So let me have this my way. Optionally lets merge Heaven and Hell with me as the supreme commander and I will in return guarantee that I will not interfere with the rest of the universe. I will drop my demand for the opening up of new markets. It will be just me, the earth, Heaven and Hell. It will be a place like no other in the universe. You visit me next eon, and you will be proud to see what I have done. I know you may not appreciate my style of functioning, but I also know you will not stop me from it. So, do we have a deal?'

'You certainly seem to be a great deal maker, Lucifer. I am impressed with your burning ambition to rule over the souls. I only wish the ambitions were diverted in a positive and creative way. You certainly have created in Hell, a very efficient, well-organized, hi-tech space with well-established controls and recognizable reward and punishment schemes. Your hierarchies and structure of control and reporting would match those of the best run companies. Your control rooms and work-flow assemblies are impressive. However all of this has only created a well-oiled inhuman machinery in a large inescapable jail with each soul being a cog in the wheel and you seemingly being the end beneficiary of whatever output the machinery is achieving. The working conditions are no different from those in a slave-driven empire that is out to create magnificent monuments for the king or the queen. What is missing is freedom. Freedom of thought, of speech, of expression! What is missing are smiles and laughter, joy and happiness, creativity and experimentation. No, this is the antithesis of all that I stand for. I was aware when you left Heaven, that you would venture out and create your own empire. I wasn't surprised when you started dabbling with earth. It was after all the work space with which all of you were familiar. You saw an opportunity in weaning away souls to Hell and creating what you believed was competition for Heaven. In corporate terms you did well. You managed a larger market share, as consultants would have you believe. You got Peter worried and you have ambitions of acquiring the remaining "business" by fair or foul means. But let me remind you that Heaven is not a business organization. It is not there to push for market shares. What we want to achieve cannot be achieved by deals being made in Heaven or in Hell. What has to be done and achieved has to be done on earth. Heaven is only a crucible for research and development, for thinkers and creators, for designing and experimenting on life forms and living styles in the universe. The focus is on how the living experience can be bettered while preserving diversity. How pluralism can be celebrated and divergent thought processes encouraged, how harmony can be sought and achieved in a chaotic world, and how laws of nature can be simplified or even eliminated to reduce regulation and controls. I want the results to help in change and development in other parts of the universe. I want a free mind, free souls. Unless you are promising me that, there can be no deal.'

'Oh God! This is all philosophy,' retorts Lucifer. 'The reality is all about power. It's about control. It's about imposing your will on all those poor souls. Yes, it's better to rule in Hell then serve in Heaven.'

'It's not about ruling, Lucifer. It's about serving. For you it's all a power game. The purpose of life is to love, serve, be of value to others, and not to control, command and conquer.'

'You do not realize the value I have created in a brand called Hell. Today if souls do opt for Hell it has to do with my life-time investment in creating an intellectual property supported by marketing. I am today able to enter minds, influence thoughts and attract souls. They will abide by all I say. My word is all that matters. All of this cannot happen overnight. It happens because of the value I offer.'

'Your so-called value, Lucifer, is limited to targeting greed, the basic instincts and the senses. Your value is ethereal. There is no real value. Just a perception.'

'Isn't that better than your own value created out of fear. Your emissaries have drilled into human minds the fear that if they do not obey your law they would go to Hell. You created Hell as a fear factor, which it is not. It is a valid choice. A legitimate post-life option that should be available to each soul. By speaking of fires in Hell and pain and suffering you have tried to persuade denizens into following stupid religions and their even stupider leaders, of living meaningless lives in prayers, a form of sycophancy that possibly makes you feel good; all in the hope of finding a place in Heaven. Your emissaries even offer virgins in Heaven to attract young males to carry out tasks on your behalf. Now you blame all of that on wayward religious groups or on me. Despite all your falsehoods I wonder why on earth would anyone want or desire a place in Heaven when there is a better option in Hell. Now that your market share has started to decline you are sitting up and taking a serious look at Hell. A place you ignored, a place you wanted all to abhor, based on fabricated lies about my kingdom. Now when I use the same marketing techniques to influence minds you call it unfair. I think it is enlightenment. The human mind is today better informed of the choices it has, it has a better understanding of afterlife and is likely to choose the option that serves its interests best, not a choice that serves your interest.'

'This is the fabled pot calling the kettle black. Fear was never a factor used in Heaven's marketing strategy. True, some religious leaders have misused religion to serve their personal interest. They are effectively working as your emissaries under the garb of my ambassadors. They are serving your needs, competently convinced by your marketing team. Heaven believes in fair play.

'Frankly the value that either Heaven or Hell holds is just in the mind. While brands do command high valuations even without matching assets, it's a bubble if the trust in the brand is lost. Let's be clear, whatever we say the brand bubble has reached a stage where people have started questioning the existence of Heaven and Hell. Your existence and mine! This is what I had desired. This is the way I want it. That the mind should evolve enough to question its origin, its existence, its nature. Now that it has started questioning and coming to more rational conclusions it finds us both to be actually the creation of the mind. We exist only in the mind. We do not exist beyond it. I did not create the mind. The mind created me and you. Historically, the cumulative power of misled minds have deliberately affirmed the existence of the non-existing. The imagined is now perceived to be the real.'

'Why do you call it unreal? You are sitting here in Hell and talking to me aren't you. Isn't that for real?'

'It is real only if thoughts in the mind of the writer and reader are real. Real only to the extent that these thoughts are penned or printed on paper. Much of what is not perceived can be real and most of what is imagined is unreal. The fact is that you and I do not exist. Only the Brand God and Brand Devil exist. Only the Brand Heaven and Brand Hell exist. But we both know there exists no such place much as we would like to believe it. However it suits us best if minds do believe in them. We have fooled people for far too long. It is time we came clean. It is time we stood up and said: We do not exist. Don't believe in us. Don't trust our emissaries. What you really need to believe is in yourself. You may listen to stories about Heaven and Hell. You may think of God and the Devil. But these are stories or narratives as hundreds and thousands you hear, read or render. These are not narratives that you should allow to take over your lives, to determine your behaviour, your decision making any more than you let other stories influence your life. I am the creator and I am the destroyer. I am Brahma the creator and Mahesh the destroyer. It is perhaps time that we self destruct ourselves. It is time to dissolve Heaven and Hell as Enterprises, concepts and lies. It is time to tell the truth. It is time to let the world know the reality. I know you would like to retain your empire, to live in the make-believe world, to retain your hold over the minds, but as one perceived to be the embodiment of Truth, of Love, of Hope I need to set the record straight. I need to let people know that we do not exist, that I do not exist. I do not want to be a placebo to mankind. To give them false hopes that I am there to help them. Yet, I do not want them to lose hope or be under the misconception that you exist and I do not. For the future of mankind lies in the hope that good exists and will prevail over evil. That perception should not be lost. They have to realize and find that truth. They have to live the goodness and be good. They have their own conscience to guide them in finding the truth. I do not need to guide them. You may try and mislead them but I believe the world will be a better place if we cease to be the guiding icons in their lives, perceived as reward and punishment. The carrot and stick are not what should determine behaviour. Good values and principles should. So tell me if you are willing to extinguish yourself the way I am ready to do. Of course, I could argue that I can terminate you the way I created you but that would be contrary to my belief that one wrong should be rectified through another wrong.'

Lucifer is furious with God for questioning their existence and even more concerned that He may self destruct a myth that serves their interests.

'Thank you for your visit,' retorts Lucifer. 'I exist as evil and am unwilling to go with your thoughts. Even the earthlings will not believe them. Some lies are best allowed to be believed. Good day.'

❄❄❄

Back in Heaven

Back in Heaven Vanderschmidt briefs the Council of Gods about their visit to Hell. Vanderschmidt's briefing obviously indicates that he has been very impressed with the way Hell is organized and is operating. He does indicate that Heaven would do well to emulate the SOPs of Hell to improve functioning and efficiency. He also talks about the strong marketing campaign of Hell targeted at the youth who are the future clients. He believes that investing early in the earthlings and capturing the mind share is the right approach. The issue up for discussion is how a marketing strategy should be designed and implemented.

When it is brought to Vanderschmidt's notice that a new marketing strategy and campaign is presented in the R&D consultancy report and the same should be the starting point of discussion, Vanderschmidt indicates his reservations about the report. He discloses to a shocked Council of Gods that the report is largely fabricated. Earthlings cannot be trusted. Even the partner of R&D who wrote the report is in Hell post his accidental or negligent death. He tells them about Ronald choosing Hell and how he admitted that R&D did not have enough time to research and had no access to Heaven or Hell about which they were advising. Given the deadlines, a financially lucrative assignment, a non-demanding client who had little knowledge of reports, Ronald felt it was okay to cheat and present a report that looked good in form even if it was low on content.

St Peter admits sheepishly that he is very disappointed with the whole R&D episode and apologizes to the Council of Gods for misleading them based on a report he believed was an outcome of extensive research.

Everyone seems shocked and they all look towards God for guidance.

God states that he was aware all along about what was happening. He did not attempt to stop or correct Peter, as He wanted to see how things would unfold. The visit to Hell did not surprise Him one bit. God says, 'Hell is doing things right, but is not doing the right thing. In Heaven we are doing the right thing though it may be argued that we are not doing it the right way. That is in a way Heaven's strength. It works democratically, allows free thought and expression, which implicitly means multiple suggestions, options and solutions, which is a recipe for greater chaos as also a bigger management challenge. Hell operates using fear as its tool and not dialogue. Hell allows no expression which therefore gives one the impression of a very homogenous, well-organized, well-functioning institution though that is highly misleading and completely incorrect. Unfortunately the leader of Hell, in the absence of free speech and expression, lives under the impression that all is well with Hell.

'I see Hell having the recipe to implode,' adds God, 'It's only a question of time. As regards the marketing success of Hell, that is true.

'We need to remember that the purpose of relocating human population to Heaven was essentially to study the evolutionary process in a non-conflict scenario. It was also to free the mind from the worries of daily survival and to focus energies on better understanding of the universe, its various life forms, the various interactions and forces at work.

'During my travels I discovered this beautiful planet, which is now called Heaven. It was so perfect, so beautiful and yet no higher life form had evolved on it. It had all the ingredients needed for evolution of the highest form of life. What was missing however was the key ingredient to evolution, the struggle for survival. Heaven was so large, so abundantly full of resources that the plant and animal life was slow to evolve in the absence of a struggle for survival. Another interesting feature that I noticed was that the life forms that had evolved in Heaven continued to live almost forever. There seemed to be no notion of death as seen in other evolved life forms on other planets. I wondered what would happen in a perfectly harmonious planet like Heaven if life could be without death. I was wondering if such a thing was at all feasible or likely. It certainly was not evolving anywhere in the universe, but the fact that life spans on Heaven were tending to infinity gave us hope. Yet over billions of earth years nothing more happened. And then as life on earth continued to evolve, and the struggle became increasingly competitive and mankind emerged from the apes and started communicating, I had this bright idea. It emerged from the prayers of people that there was a fear of death. Mankind was obsessed with death as no other creature anywhere in the universe. Mankind was mortified at the concept of death and the wonderment of what happens after death. The number of prayers for an afterlife in a safe place where there was no conflict, no struggle, abundance of resources and life in perpetuity kept on mounting. I thought, why not transpose the earthlings post death to Heaven. That way I could populate Heaven instead of waiting endlessly to see and study how life would evolve. Now the transposition was not possible in the human form owing to Heaven being light years away from earth. So I decided that I would move only the soul, the energy form that exists in the body, which can travel at speeds of light and transpose those to Heaven. I could allow a body-feel to the soul that would ensure a comfort level to the soul and there need be no relearning in the new avatar. As the population in Heaven grew, I had to appoint the more capable souls to manage the affairs of Heaven. Thus came about the angels. Some of these were sent back to earth to retrain humans on earth as the quality of humans coming to Heaven was poor. My emissaries who went to earth to retrain and improve the humans were actually harassed, hounded and even killed. I did not want a planet where everyone was expected to live in peace to be interrupted by undesirable elements. I therefore had to introduce measures. A kind of visa for Heaven you may say. And only the selected ones who had lived on earth the way I would like them to live in Heaven were admitted. The others were left to spin off in space as energy plasmas until Hell happened. Lucifer opted out and decided to set up his own empire. Lucifer soon became Satan and set up camp at this hot planet called Hell. He decided to populate it with all the evil souls and ended up choosing all those who failed to find entry into Heaven. He even started a marketing campaign to win over the better humans to dedicate their souls to Hell. He actually started creating Hell in mind spaces on earth and many humans started living their Hell on earth itself. It was extremely unfortunate that we could not influence enough human minds through the emissaries who were sent to earth. They tried hard. What emerged however was shocking. The teachings of the emissaries were twisted and modified by humans calling themselves preachers, pundits, priests or mullahs, and they codified the preachings as it suited them and used them to their advantage to gain dominance over the minds of others.

'I am happy that a large amount of work has been done by scientists, researchers and others in Heaven, to understand natural forces, their origin and their impact through interaction not just in Heaven, but across the universe. I am happy that a large number of pioneers have ventured out to the remotest parts of the universe and come back with very valuable information, data and reports. I am delighted that the arts, music, performances, holograms have blossomed so well and enrichened the experience of those living in Heaven. I am pleased with the way architecture, town planning, services have grown. It is heartening that there are no conflicts, no negativism and no insecurities in Heaven.'

St Peter informs God that there is a major campaign on earth that propagates that jihadis who fight in the name of God will find martyrdom in Heaven. In reality the jihadis are killing people believing that they will be rewarded for a deed they are supposed to be committing on behalf of God. He rues the fact that such canards cannot be stopped with all the power available to Heaven. He suspects that the Devil is behind the campaign and is actually taking away the jihadis to Hell when they get killed or die, although on earth they are celebrated as martyrs who have reached God.

'I am happy,' says God, 'that my different ambassadors sent to earth from time to time have seeded thought processes that allow pluralistic thinking and interpretations. In any case, the creation and the creator are far too complex and multilayered for the human mind, which is in its early development stages, to be interpreted in any linear mode. The problem however lies in a non-scientific interpretation that is manipulated to the advantage of the interpreter in his effort to gain power and undue advantage. The interpreters usurp positions in the religious hierarchies claiming proximity to me, which allows them to remain unchallenged and thereby adds force to their interpretations. The interpretations need to sound extreme and need to be supported by permissible drastic action in case of a failure of the followers to abide by the interpretation. Such coercive action helps create the monsters, who while promising Heaven are doomed to go to Hell along with their followers.

'Happily, I see that most people are not influenced by the extremists. True, the few who are influenced by the extremists can wreck havoc among the innocent moderates. All through the ages, whether it's the crusaders or the jihadis, they have believed erroneously that their salvation lay in their misdeeds. I want the mind to challenge these beliefs and to evolve into saner creatures.

'I have experimented with various forms of life. Let us look at Heaven itself. It has not evolved. There has been little motivation for evolution. Life is far too comfortable in Heaven with unlimited resources, unlimited time; yet when you look at earth with all its problems, that is where innovation is happening. Change is occurring and experimentation is taking place. Motivation comes from conflict, from insecurity, from competition. Change comes through death, which is the best thing that evolution could have invented. Death leads to new life being born. Where there is death there is life. In fact, except for a few pockets in the universe the rest of it is lifeless.

'I have experimented in other galaxies life forms where such conflicts do not exist and find that evolution of the mind in such situations is slow. Defining the right path, continuously reviewing what is right and what is wrong, challenging those on a path considered wrong at that point in time, even at the risk of life, are among the physical and intellectual needs of growth and evolution. That is the beauty of human life, which I do not see in other forms of creation. True, it is accompanied by a fair amount of violence, where the earthlings are sending people back to Heaven or Hell earlier than I had designed, but the shift in location or the transition of one life form and its elements into another is a small price to pay for what results in a movement towards the better. I see that happening—though in time frames of earth that may be slow, in Heavenly time frames that is fairly good.

'It should not be our effort to market Heaven and add to external din. What we need to do is ensure that the inner voice gets better heard in the plethora of external noises.

'During the research by R&D earthlings have not been asked the right questions. Hell and Heaven should not be something they should choose from when they die. It should be something they should make while on earth. What they make on earth is what decides their transition. If one has made one's own life hell and those of others around too then one is best prepared to be in Hell. To enter Heaven one must do on earth what is needed to make each one's own earthly existence a paradise. To do that you have to be able to dispel evil in every form: anger, envy, jealousy, sorrow, regret, greed, arrogance, self pity, guilt, resentment, inferiority, lies, false pride, superiority, and ego; and nurture the good, i.e., joy, peace, love, hope, serenity, humility, kindness, benevolence, empathy, generosity, truth, compassion, and faith.'

The gods plead with God to use his powers and miraculously resolve all issues. God says, 'Evolution and the rules that guide it are the miracles. Every interactivity works on defined principles labelled by earthlings as science. There is no such thing as a miracle. Miracles are defined by earthlings as inexplicable happenings that they are ready to believe in the absence of understanding the event. It is not the miracle but the ignorance that is at display. There has been some amount of understanding among earthlings of the nano, sub-micro, micro and mega particles and forces that make creation work. It's a good beginning and credit must go to the seekers of truth, researchers and scientists. There is however still a long way to go. The more the earthlings understand creation, the less will they believe in miracles and in me. There should be no scope for illogical beliefs. There would be no control over evolution and what follows if there were no defined laws to govern the particles, forces, interaction that is responsible for all visible and invisible happenings. The lack of understanding does lead people to give credit to me for being responsible for miracles. But no, I cannot claim credit for mankind's ignorance or the refusal to understand the truth. If I am God, it is because I am the ultimate scientist who understood that only well defined laws would create a harmonious universe. You do see the Devil changing goalposts mid stream and applying laws differently. It is that vagary that is responsible for a chaotic Hell even if it superficially looks very organized.'

The gods are all aghast at learning that there are no miracles and God does not intervene and refuses to acknowledge that he created the universe. He just lets the forces operate as per the laws defined. So does that mean that everything is predecided and works as per the forces and their properties?

'No,' says God as if reading the minds of the gods. 'The uncertainty principle that allows some level of unpredictability in the time-space motion of the non-living matter and the unpredictability of the MIND among the living, ensures that nothing is predetermined. The power of the mind varies from species to species with the human mind being among the most evolved on earth. If this uncertainty did not exist then people would be mere puppets of forces and everything would be predictable. Life itself would be meaningless.

'In fact, one of the things that the Devil has done is take away the MIND from a lot of people. This has made things fairly predictable for the mindless. Yes, many people are happy with this predictability and the absence of any effort needed to take a decision. But they are reduced to the status of the non living. It is better to be a living being with uncertainty in Heaven than have certainty in Hell but no choice or the ability to choose. The absence of predictability has ensured that even God cannot be sure of how the future will unfold. People generally believe that God knows the future. Yes, God is aware of the general direction in which the world is moving, but has done away with absolute predictability to make life more interesting. The uncertainty principle has given life a new dimension and meaning. Predictability would have meant taking away the possibility of life determining its own direction.

'Before we find a solution, let us understand a few facts about life, its origin and its existence. Let me step out of the narrative created over hundreds and thousands of years. A narrative created by the minds of humans. Humans who needed a story to cling on to, a hero to look up to, a super power to solve their problems, and finally, to keep them from destroying themselves.

'The narrative created a super power, one that no one quite understood. One that was omnipotent, omnipresent, yet cannot be seen. One that was never born, never can die, never can cease. One who cannot be challenged. Not just me but all of you are the creation of such a narrative.

'Now in a unique role reversal I, the principal character created in the narrative, wherein I am supposed to have created everything, shall step out of the narrative and find myself looking at a wonderful universe. My thoughts, as I see this real world and realize that I am the only unreal part therein, are that I did not create the universe. I did not create life. Life evolved. I did nothing. The nano particle was virtually a tiny microscopic speck of high concentrated energy that could split in different ways to give rise to more nano particles such as photons, protons, electrons, neutrons, bosons, fermions, etc. Creating a complex universe would essentially need a very simple process. All that was needed was a building block which for the moment lets call the origion. Now to create the enormous universe one would have needed googleions of origions. The simplest way to do that would be to create just the prototype nano particle that could replicate itself infinitely. So the prototype would keep replicating itself and each new origion again would keep replicating endlessly. Since it would take only milliseconds for an origion to replicate itself, it was only a question of a few billion earth years for gazillions and googleions of nano particles to be born. To ensure that the replication does not go on infinitely a built-in clock that ensures that post a critical mass the particles would stop replicating on their own would be needed. The other feature of the origion is that they attract each other when they spin close to each other and the circle of spin keeps on diminishing and the bonds of attraction increase, so that as they come closer, they spin faster, attract each other more and finally collide to merge, releasing large amounts of energy. Each merged pair merges with other merged pairs and so on, till the mergers reach massive proportions to create atoms, molecules and elements that then grow into masses of an infinite size. Finally the entity became so enormous with an infinite diameter, infinite density and infinite mass that it imploded and then in one massive Big Bang, exploded to send out enormous amounts of material and energies outwards leading to billions of galaxies being formed with each galaxy having billions of stars and planets. That is perhaps how the universe originated. The issue of the origin of the nano particles with some interesting characteristics from energy fluxes is still being researched. Among the interesting characteristics were conversion from energy to matter and vice versa, the spin, the gravitational force and the uncertainty principle.

'That I was in any way responsible for the origin of the universe is totally untrue. It is however true that the particles emerged out of nothing. Zilch. Zero. Just as it is possible to split zero into a positive value and a negative value, so too out of nothingness were born the positive and the negative nano particles.

'Interestingly there were certain specifications in some parts of the universe that favoured the emergence of the groupings that demonstrated characteristics of life and later got to be called organisms, that had life, that could contribute to determining their own future. The specifications were later, fairly accurately, identified by Mark Rees and the band of Goldilock indicated areas in the Solar Systems where life was most likely to evolve.

'Rees' six numbers is the magnitude of the so-called force, the force that binds the component of the nucleus.

'The value of the force determines the kind of combination of atomic particles that is possible. Different combinations lead to the creation of different elements with differing properties. If the force whose value in the universe were different the universe may have contained nothing but hydrogen and no interesting elements or variations that could have led to the creation of ingredients needed for life. If the force was somewhat larger in value then the hydrogen would have fused to make heavier elements and there could be no hydrogen, which is so very vital for the creation of water and of life. The Goldilocks value is perfect for the creation of life. The other numbers pointed out by Rees explain similarly that had the forces or the compositions been even a little different life would not have emerged. Interestingly the numbers all converge in the Goldilocks band in the universe, which is where life is most likely to be found. That includes the planet earth. So if one was to look for life in other parts of the universe one has to look in the Goldilocks band. I am happy that both Rees and Goldilocks continue to do very valuable research in Heaven. Their research, which is available on Hoogle, is used by many adventurous space travellers and time travellers to venture out to study the different species.

'The emergence of life and its evolution over time from simple protozoas to highly complex humans has been explained by scientists over the years. As the organisms evolved and as the mind emerged, it set in motion what was to be the ultimate triumph, the creation of homo sapiens. It was now only a matter of time before the evolution could reach a stage where the evolved species could think. In the real narrative as it unfolded, I was all throughout the Nothingness, the emptiness. I was the Nothing out of which emerged the first replicable nano particles. That was all that was needed for the universe to emerge and for life to evolve, just one replicable particle that could merge with its twin and continue replicating and continue merging. Creating such a simple particle did not require a God or any God. It needed flux of energy and the unique set of forces. It is however so much easier for a narration where I am created out of nothing rather than trying to understand the highly complex world of nano particles and forces of physics at work. The narrative involving me was highly simplistic and highly misleading. Yet the narration itself was good and over a period of time took on a life of its own to reach the status of acquired truth that could not be challenged.

'There is more valuable research coming out of earth relating to the origin of the universe, the emergence of life, the nature of the universe, the Pendulum theory, Big Bang and Big Crunch theories.

'In the narration of Heaven so far, souls have the liberty and freedom to travel whenever, wherever at speeds of light. This allows them to physically go out to test hypothesis and bring back information or pass back information that can be meaningfully analyzed. Yet another advantage is time travel. Thus souls can travel backwards or forwards in time. This has given rise to a humongous source of information that is just not possible on earth except in fiction. They also have unlimited resources to experiment with. The whole universe is their lab. The narrative itself should therefore unfold a lot of truths and destroy many myths in the process including the myth of Heaven and Hell. But this narration is different from the generally accepted narrative of the theory of creativity.

'Even I could not have done anything that could have been anywhere close to what evolution achieved, had I attempted to create with all the attributes conferred on me by the narrative.

'The interesting thing that emerged from the evolution of the mind was that it could create, and create just about anything in a virtual world including the universe, and it could actually lead itself into believing what it had created. One such creation of the mind was me. So, yes, while I did not create the universe, the mind created me. I really do not exist, neither does the Devil nor do any of you. Some of you did exist at some point in time and do carry a legacy but have now got merged with the unreal for even if you existed you now exist only in the minds of people who do not let you go. We are all creatures of the human mind. I have said this earlier too and I repeat, "WE DO NOT EXIST."'

All the gods are shocked to hear this. Are they only a part of a human narrative? Are they created by humans, when all along they were led to believe that they created the universe, the earth, life? Now the real and the virtual are becoming indistinguishable.

'How is it, God, that you are saying you do not exist when the very act of your saying so implies that you exist. There is a contradiction in terms.'

God explains, 'There are four forms of existence. That of the inanimate, they do not know that they exist; that of the living that know that they exist; that of empty space that does not know that it does not exist; and that of God that knows that it does not exist. For I am there, and I am not there! I exist only in the mind. I do not exist, if the mind does not believe in my existence. I am like a virtual image that does not exist and yet is there. I am like the apparition that does not exist yet you get the feeling that it is there. I am like the dream that you see but exists only in the mind. I am like a vision that inspires you but it exists only when you make it real. I exist only in the mind of the believer. I have no weight, no mass, no volume and no particles. I can be whatever the mind visualizes. I can adopt any shape, size or colour. I can be non dimensional and multidimensional. I am the space between the subatomic particles. However I am one who knows that I do not exist. How can anyone know its own non existence?

'None can, but I do, so I am God.

'I am like the zero. If you divide a finite number by zero it equals infinity. Mathematically that implies that if zero is multiplied by infinity it equals a finite number. I am the zero, the non existing, the nothingness that in an infinite space and time yields a positive finite creation—the universe. I have only three features that are different from souls. I can travel at infinite speed, I can be at all places at all times and I know that I do not exist. We all exist only in the mind. In the minds of the people, who believe in us, not in our own minds. So what we see, experience or believe is in our minds and we are dreams within dreams and virtual reality within the unreal world. What really exists is the book. I do not exist, yet I have created the universe. As you know, nothing comes from Nothing, but Nothing is analogous not digital, so the nothing that comes from Nothing is not completely and exactly the same Nothing. The variation Delta in mathematical terms is zero or tends to zero and is almost nothing. However over time spans running into not millions or billions of years, but zillions of light years and replications happening gazillions of times Nothing actually becomes something. The original Nothing is the unreal Me, the something today is the real universe or the multiverse as each universe tends to replicate over time. The original Me has evolved from Nothing into the origion, which through replication in infinite time has filled space, fused to liberate energies called stars or suns, fused further to create heavier atoms, exploded and imploded to give rise to planets and planetary systems, galaxies and universes, chemically evolved to give rise to organic life that further evolved on billions of planets including the earth to give enormously varied life and life patterns. Yes, there are today billions of billions of planets in billions of universes.

'The only instrument of creativity is the mind. Everything else is only evolutionary. External forces working according to the laws of physics will only transform the environment in stages and it is only over evolutionary time spans that things will change in small steps. The mind however is structured to think and to collease the forces of nature in a way that can unleash, transform, build differently and jump the evolutionary mechanism. So in its efforts to find the rationale behind evolutionary forces that are difficult to comprehend given its different time spans, the mind found simplistic solutions for Creation in an all powerful entity embodied in the form of God. Just as matter could be rearranged in forms that could give illusions of reality whether through the creation of moving images, holograms or 3D interactive characters, that were as ephemeral as the moments of life leading to the loss of comprehension between the real and the created, so too was the loss of the understanding where it was unclear whether God was a creation or his creation was real. So effectively the mind further created a kingdom for God and in his image his messengers, the angels and the Devil. It was an effort of trying to fit in a created hypothesis against a reality that was difficult to comprehend. As the complexity of the universal space was too intricate for a simplistic hypothesis of God to address the issues scientifically, the hypothesis underwent periodic changes until finally it became far too ridiculous to explain, yet continued to be used as no one was willing or strong enough to throw the whole hypothesis out as generation after generation had been fed on and controlled through this heavily patched-up hypothesis.

'So if you all agree, this is the time to take some hard decisions. It is time to say adieu, au revoir. It is time to tell the world to wake up and live for today. It is time for them to create Heaven on earth. Let the world live, let us end our world.

'Shall we resolve to self terminate the God delusion? Shall we press Ctrl + Alt + Delete and end the myth?'

***

Glossary

3D	Three Dimension
Multi-D	Multi Dimensional
HD	High Definition
M&A	Mergers and Acquisitions
CEO	Chief Executive Officer
PE Ratio	Price to Equity Ratio (it helps determine the company's perceived value)
WSJ	*Wall Street Journal*
NDA	Non Disclosure Agreement (a confidentiality requirement in deal making)
TG	Target Group (for research or marketing)
USD	US Dollar
VAT	Value Added Tax
VP	Vice President
SOP	Standard Operating Procedure (set rules of operation)
MIS	Management Information System (a tool to help senior management to evaluate performance)
AV	Audio Visual
SWOT	Strength, Weakness, Opportunity, Threat (a system of evaluating a company's strengths)
IT	Information Technology